FOR SERVICES RENDERED

Ann Patrick

A KISMET™ Romance

METEOR PUBLISHING CORPORATION
Bensalem, Pennsylvania

To Kate Duffy, a great editor.

Special thanks to a terrific critique group:
Susan Brown, Betty Gyenes, Elaine Kimberley,
Heather MacAllister, and Alaina Richardson.

ANN PATRICK

Ann Patrick has had a lifelong love affair with books. Other loves are shopping, collecting elephants, movies, Broadway shows, Calvin & Hobbs, music, the company of her family and friends, traveling, and animals (especially cats). She and her husband live in Houston, Texas, and have three grown children.

Other KISMET books by Ann Patrick:

ONE

Claire Kendrick shifted in her chair and nervously glanced at her watch. She'd been waiting twenty minutes, and the longer she waited, the more fidgety and irritated she became. Why had Nick Callahan sent for her? she asked herself for at least the twelfth time. Was something wrong? Was someone dissatisfied with her work?

Surely not. She was doing an excellent job in the public relations department of Callahan, International. Besides, even if there *was* something wrong with her work, her supervisor would have called her in—not the president of the company.

Claire looked up. Rain sluiced across the bank of windows of the 50th-floor office and thunder rumbled nearby. She could barely see the fuzzy outlines of the other downtown buildings through the low-hanging gunmetal clouds. Houston in January could be as miserable as any northern city, she thought.

"Miss Kendrick?"

Claire turned.

Nick Callahan's secretary beckoned. "Mr. Callahan will see you now."

About time, Claire thought, relieved that she'd finally find out what was going on. The older woman led Claire down a short hall, through a set of double walnut doors, and into a massive corner office.

"Miss Kendrick is here, Mr. Callahan," said the secretary.

"Thank you, Wanda," he answered without looking up.

Wanda disappeared noiselessly across the thick pile of gray carpeting. Claire stood uncertainly in front of the enormous glass-topped oak desk. Nick Callahan scrawled on the top sheet of the stack of papers in front of him. Then he put them aside, and his dark head lifted. Brilliant blue eyes studied her, and in spite of her repeated assurances to herself that she had nothing to worry about, she couldn't help the sudden flutter of nerves that gripped her.

"Please have a seat, Miss Kendrick." His voice was low, the words clipped. He gestured in the direction of several burgundy suede chairs grouped on the right side of his desk. "Shall I ask Wanda to bring you some coffee or tea?"

"No, thank you." Claire sat and arranged her navy wool skirt neatly. Whatever this interview was about, she just wanted it to be over quickly.

"Sorry to have kept you waiting," he said.

She shrugged. The thought flitted through her mind that he was better looking than she'd expected. From all the stories she'd heard about him, she'd expected someone who looked like a prizefighter. Instead, Nick Callahan looked as if he'd be more at home on the ski slopes than in the ring—fit and trim and tanned. He appeared to be tall, but since he was seated, it was impossible to tell. Thick, dark hair—expertly cut and styled—framed a strong, angular face. He wore an expensive-looking navy pinstriped suit, a glistening white shirt, and a dark red silk tie. Even if she hadn't known he was the president of a multi-billion dollar corporation, she would have known he was somebody. Everything about him suggested power and wealth.

The startling blue of his eyes fascinated her. They were totally unexpected, an incongruity. His was a face that should have had brooding dark eyes, she thought.

He tapped his pencil against the desk and continued to study her thoughtfully. Claire's stomach muscles tensed under his unwavering scrutiny, and even though she sat quietly, not saying anything, the same irritation she'd felt over being kept waiting crept back. What was this? Intimidation by staring? Well, two could play this game. She lifted her chin and stared back, even though there was uneasiness under her bravado.

Soft chimes broke the silence, and her eyes were drawn to the onyx clock gracing the oak credenza behind him: 11:00.

Finally he said, "Miss Kendrick, I've been investigating your work."

Before she could formulate an answer to this surprising statement, there was a sharp rap on the door, followed by the sound of someone entering the room.

"Come on in, Tim," Callahan said. "Miss Kendrick, I've asked Tim Sutherland, my staff administrator, to sit in on our meeting."

Claire turned, watching as Tim Sutherland advanced into the room, stopping directly in front of her.

"No, don't get up," he said when she started to

stand. After shaking her hand, he sat in one of the burgundy chairs facing her. "Sorry I'm a bit late." He smoothed back a stray lock of light brown hair. He was a stocky man who looked to be in his middle thirties. He had dark brown eyes and a pleasant looking, square face covered with freckles. Claire remembered having seen him in the halls.

"No problem," Nick Callahan said. Picking up a thin green folder from the center of his desk, he returned his attention to Claire and said, "This is your personnel file. I've studied it thoroughly, and I believe you're the ideal person for a special assignment I have in mind."

"An assignment?" What kind of assignment would warrant the president of the company and his right-hand man talking to her about it instead of Betty O'Neill, the director of Claire's department?

"You have an impressive background," Callahan continued, ignoring her question as he flipped open the folder and ran his index finger down a sheet of paper clipped inside her file. "Valedictorian of your high school graduating class, Jesse H. Jones scholarship, summa cum laude graduate of the University of Texas, first-rate work with the Middleton Foundation, an outstanding portfolio. . . ."

"Thank you," she murmured.

He looked up, his gaze direct and unblinking. "I read the article you wrote about Dr. Middleton, too. It was excellent." Turning to Tim Sutherland, he said, "You thought so, too, didn't you, Tim?"

Sutherland nodded. "Yes. It was very good."

Sutherland didn't smile and his praise seemed almost reluctant. Puzzled, Claire said, "Thank you, but I wrote that article years ago. How did you happen to see it, Mr. Callahan?"

"I have my sources."

Was that a glimmer of amusement in his eyes?

He closed the file and leaned back in his chair. "Miss Kendrick, I've been approached by *C.E.O.* magazine. They want to publish a profile on me."

Claire wasn't surprised that the magazine, one that had been giving *Forbes* and *Entrepreneur* a run for their money, was interested in featuring Nick Callahan. He'd made his first million before he was thirty, and Callahan, International—once a small construction company with a few dozen employees—now had over 20,000 employees worldwide. It was also a Fortune 500 company with a triple A Dun & Bradstreet rating. Claire had done some investigating herself before accepting the position with them three months ago. She'd had to. In her situation, she couldn't afford to make a mistake.

"I've told the *C.E.O.* people the only way I would consent to this story is if one of my own people wrote it." He paused for half a heartbeat. "That's where you come in."

"Me?" Claire could have kicked herself for not being able to hide her incredulity.

"Yes, you. I want you to write the story."

"Why?"

He gave her a startled look, which he quickly disguised. "Why not?" he countered.

Confused by his reaction but trying not to show it, she ticked off the reasons. "All my training and experience are in public relations. I write great press releases and copy for brochures—that kind of thing—but I have no experience doing personal interviews or in-depth features for magazines.''

"Exactly what I told him," Tim Sutherland interjected.

"You did the one on Dr. Middleton," Nick Callahan said, meeting her gaze and completely ignoring Sutherland's remark.

"That was different. Dr. Middleton is an old family friend. I did the story as a favor to him."

"Well, do this story as a favor to me."

As he spoke, lightning sizzled across the dark sky and the lights in the office flickered. For a moment Claire watched the storm outside as she searched for an appropriate rejoinder. When her gaze returned to his, her uneasiness intensified. She had a strong sense there was something Nick Callahan wasn't telling her. She told herself she was being silly, but the feeling refused to go away. Taking a deep breath, Claire said carefully, "Mr. Callahan, I'm flattered to be asked, but you and I both know I'm not the best person for this assignment."

"We disagree."

Claire glanced at Tim Sutherland. His eyes, which looked as if they should be warm and friendly to match his face, were anything but. In fact, they seemed cold and assessing, and their expression chilled Claire. It was obvious to her that Nick Callahan's use of the word *we* was a fabrication.

Perhaps he thought she was right for the job, but his administrator did not. Under the best of circumstances, an assignment like this would be a tremendous challenge. With Sutherland against her, she would be operating under a heavy disadvantage. What if she wasn't able to deliver the kind of article Nick Callahan wanted? God, she couldn't afford a screw-up. This job was too important to her. "Aren't the people at *C.E.O.* worried that a story by one of your employees would end up being just a puff piece?" she finally offered.

"It's not meant to be an exposé, it's a profile," he said.

"Still—"

"They have no choice. If they want the story, they'll take you. If not . . ." He shrugged. "No story." Then he smiled, showing very white teeth which looked even whiter against the chiseled darkness of his face. If possible, the smile—which should have put her at ease with him—made her even more uncomfortable. There was something almost predatory in its mocking charm. He darted a look at Tim Sutherland and said smoothly, "I know what I'm doing. Trust me."

Claire looked at Sutherland, too. He looked doubtful. She sighed, the sound lost in the rising wail of the wind outside. Resigned, she said, "When do I start?"

"How does tomorrow sound?" He stood. Tim Sutherland also got to his feet. They both looked down at her.

Although her insides were jumping, Claire stood without haste. When Nick Callahan extended his hand, she took it after only a moment's hesitation. His grip was firm but not crushing, and his hand felt smooth and warm. His vivid gaze held hers for a long moment, and Claire had a sudden absurd urge to turn and run.

"Do you have any objections to traveling?" He released her hand, but his electric-blue eyes remained fastened on her face.

With difficulty, Claire concentrated on the question. She thought about her mother. "Not as long as I don't have to be gone for extended periods. I have some personal obligations that would preclude a long trip."

"I'm talking about short trips—two or three days at most."

"No, that's not a problem."

"Good. For the duration of this assignment, you'll receive your daily instructions from Tim. However, as he'll be in Tulsa for the next two days, I'd like you to report to me tomorrow morning at nine. After a briefing, I'll expect you to attend a meeting with me at ten, then you'll join me for lunch." He reeled off the instructions quickly, all business. "Any questions?"

"No." What good would it do to give voice to them?

"All right. See you in the morning then."

Dismissed, she thought. She was totally confused. She knew she wasn't the best choice for this assignment. Why, in her own department alone, she could think of two others, including her supervisor, who were more qualified to write this story. But she also knew this assignment was a tremendous opportunity for her, and if she did it well, it might pave the way for more rapid promotion within the company. She'd probably been a fool to protest.

Turning, she walked rapidly out of the office. She looked neither right nor left as she entered the reception area, passed Wanda, and let herself out of the executive suite.

Riding down in the elevator, she rehashed the entire conversation in her mind. Throughout the interview, there had been undercurrents—undercurrents Claire hadn't understood. But one thing she *did* understand.

No matter what he said, Nick Callahan was hiding something from her.

Nick stood watching as Claire Kendrick marched out of his office with a long, purposeful stride. He admired the way her pleated skirt swung against her slender, long legs and the sway of her blond hair as it shimmered like a golden curtain around her head.

His smile widened with satisfaction. From the first moment he'd set eyes on her—talking to a co-worker as he walked by—he was intrigued by her. Then, after investigating her background, he knew she had the qualities he was looking for.

Today's interview had been the clincher. Claire seemed perfect for what he had in mind. Smart. Determined. Hardworking. Loyal. And as the *pièce de résistance*, she was quite lovely, with that silky-looking, butter-colored hair and those dreamy, gray-green eyes. Her skin looked soft and smooth, as if she'd been painted in watercolors, all delicate pastels covering a canvas of underlying strength.

Well-satisfied with his initial judgment, he turned toward Tim, who had walked to the windows and stood looking out. "Well, what do you think?" Nick asked.

Tim turned, giving him a thoughtful look. "I've already told you what I think." He grimaced. "Not that you paid any attention."

"I meant, what did you think of *her*?" Nick joined Tim at the windows and they both gazed out at what was visible of Houston's downtown area through the heavy rain. While they watched, lightning zigzagged across the charcoal sky.

"What I think of her is irrelevant," Tim said, a note of exasperation in his voice, "because I know you. When you decide to do something, it doesn't matter to you what anyone else thinks. You do it anyway."

Nick smiled. He *was* stubborn when he thought he was right, although tenacious was the term he preferred. His tenacity was the reason he usually got what he wanted, he thought with satisfaction. Because once he set a goal, he didn't let anything deter him from reaching it.

"But I can't help feeling there's something you're not telling me about this situation," Tim said.

Tim was no fool. And because he was Nick's friend as well as his legal counsel and right-hand man, Nick considered telling Tim the whole truth. But things might not work out, and if they didn't, it would be best for both Nick and Claire Kendrick that no one know what he was considering. "You're imagining things," he said mildly. But he couldn't meet Tim's eyes.

"All right, have it your own way. I've known you long enough to realize you'll tell me when you're ready to tell me and not a moment sooner. But, Nick . . ."

Nick turned. Tim was frowning. For just a second, Nick felt a flicker of unease, but quickly dismissed it. Tim's prudence and cautiousness, which were two of his greatest assets, could also be his greatest weaknesses. Nick had learned long ago that a successful business coup required boldness, even a certain arrogance. You made your plan, then you stuck to it, using whatever tactic seemed to work best. The only time he'd ever failed was when he'd allowed emotions to rule his actions. He had no intention of ever repeating that mistake.

"Whatever this is about, just be careful," Tim finished darkly.

Claire tapped softly on Betty O'Neill's office door.
"Come in."

"Well," said Betty as Claire entered the cluttered office, "what did Mr. Magnificent want?"

"Is that what you call him?"

Betty laughed. "Among other things. After all, the guy's got everything. Black Irish charm, Russian intelligence, tons of money." As she spoke, she ticked the items off on her fingers. Her eyes twinkled. "And he positively oozes sex appeal!"

Claire gave her a mock frown, although it was hard to resist Betty's gamine charm. A tiny woman with dark hair and lively hazel eyes, she had an irresistibly cheery approach to life that Claire both admired and envied. "He *is* attractive," she reluctantly admitted, "but he's scary, too." She hesitated, feeling foolish. "He reminds me of a highwayman."

Betty chuckled, then pointed to her coffee. "Want some?"

"No, thanks."

Betty leaned forward, her eyes full of curiosity. "Tell me what he said."

"He's asked me to take on a special assignment."

"An assignment? Why didn't he come through me?"

Claire repeated what she'd been told during the interview. "Funny, isn't it?"

Betty frowned. "Yes."

"He said the reason I was chosen is that I've done an article similar to this in the past." She gave Betty a brief rundown on the Middleton article, trying to make it sound as if this new assignment were perfectly logical, even as her mind told her it wasn't.

Betty took a sip of her ever-present cup of coffee. A knowing glint in her eye, she said, "If I didn't know that he never dates employees, my guess would be he's interested in you."

"Interested in me!" Claire felt her skin growing hot. Blast it! What was wrong with her that she let her feelings show no matter what she was thinking? Why couldn't she be cool like other women managed to be? Like Peachey Hall, her best friend, would have been? Claire hated the trait that made her wear her emotions like so much costume jewelry, obvious to all. "That's ridiculous."

"Why is it ridiculous?"

"It just is." Claire knew she must look like a lobster, blushing furiously. "A man like Nick Callahan can have his pick of women. He'd certainly never pick someone like me."

"I happen to disagree. In fact, if you *weren't* an employee, I can't imagine him *not* being interested in you. Any man with eyes would be."

"Oh, Betty . . ." Claire always felt uncomfortable when people complimented her. Peachey had once told her the mark of a gracious woman was the ability to receive a compliment with poise.

"Just say, thank you, and be done with it," she'd advised Claire.

"But to my knowledge he's never dated any of the women who work for the company," Betty continued. "And it's not because they haven't tried."

Yes, Claire could see why women would go after Nick Callahan. As Betty had said earlier, he had everything going for him. Even now, thinking about those eyes of his gave her an unsettled feeling. "You don't think he's setting me up for something, do you, Betty?" Claire asked, giving voice to the niggling fear she'd tried to push down.

"Like what?"

"I don't know. It's just that something isn't quite right about all this, and it's driving me crazy trying to figure it out."

"You know, Claire, you may as well relax," Betty

said. "Knowing what I know about our CEO, even if he has some ulterior motive in choosing you for this assignment, you're not going to find out what it is until he's good and ready to enlighten you—and not one minute sooner."

Claire stood. "You're probably right. I'd better use my energy to do a good job."

Betty smiled. "That's the ticket."

Claire smiled back. "I feel better already. Thanks, Betty."

"Don't mention it. But, Claire . . ." Betty hesitated. "Be careful. Don't go falling for him."

Claire laughed self-consciously. "Don't worry. I'm not stupid. There's absolutely no chance of that happening."

Nick idly observed the well-dressed, noisy crowd from his vantage point at the far end of Heather Richardson's sumptuous living room. He propped his arm on the marble mantel as he watched her graceful approach. Under his breath, he murmured to Tim, "The queen cometh."

Tim laughed. "She *does* like to rule. And she thinks you and your kingdom are next in line."

Fat chance, Nick thought. He had no intention of falling into that kind of trap. Once was enough. Not that he harbored any ill feelings toward his ex-wife. Jill hadn't tried to deceive him. She'd never pretended to be anything other than what she was—a spoiled, pampered, self-centered woman. It wasn't her fault he'd ignored what his brain was telling him and married her anyway. He grimaced. By becoming besotted with Jill, he'd lost his edge. He'd no longer been able to think clearly. And it had cost him. His personal life had become a battleground, affecting his entire life.

"Darling," Heather said, gliding next to Nick and sliding her pale, bare arm behind his back. She rubbed her face against his dinner jacket, and he caught a whiff of her perfume, something heavy and sensuous. "Why are you hiding out over here? You look so dark and brooding, like Heathcliff, or something. Come join the rest of us."

"I'm just tired, Heather," Nick said.

"Oh, pooh." She adopted her little girl look—the one that was coy and flirtatious—the one she thought would get her anything she wanted. "You're *always* tired. You never want to do anything." She tossed her thick mane of red-gold hair.

"I work hard."

"I know that. But you have to play, too."

Now she batted her eyelashes, and Nick groaned inwardly. The mannerisms he'd thought so charming when he'd first started dating her had worn thin. Even her beautiful, thick eyelashes masking tawny eyes no longer had the power to sway him.

"Tim, you tell him . . ." Heather wheedled. "All work and no play will make Nicky a *very* dull boy."

"You're a very dull boy," Tim said obediently, his brown eyes dancing with amusement. "How about me, Heather? Will I do as a playmate?"

"Oh, you!" She reached up, planting a kiss in the middle of Nick's mouth. "Don't leave early. I'm looking forward to spending the wee hours alone with you."

Nick resisted the urge to wipe his mouth with the back of his hand. It was long past time to break off with her. "I can't stay tonight, Heather. I've got an early meeting in the morning."

Heather's smooth brow wrinkled, and her voice hardened. "I'm getting the idea I'm not very important to you, Nick. Is that true?"

"Of course you're important to me," Nick hedged.

"Then prove it. Stay tonight."

Nick sighed. "I'm sorry, Heather. I really can't."

"Well, in that case, I'll just to have to find someone who can!" She whirled around and in a swish of emerald taffeta, walked away, head held high.

"Methinks the lady's angry, milord," Tim said. He brushed his hair out of his eyes.

Nick knew he'd hurt Heather's feelings and that disgusted him. After all, what had she done that was so terrible? She'd behaved exactly the way she'd always behaved; he was just tired of her. That wasn't her fault and she didn't deserve this kind of treatment. Always before, when he'd broken off a liaison, he'd treated the woman fairly—been open and honest with her. He'd prided himself on his ability to break off his relationships without hard feelings. He usually just bought the woman in question something expensive—such as a new mink coat or a pair of ruby earrings—said all the right things to salve her hurt feelings—and all would be forgiven. In fact, he was still friends with most of the women he'd been linked with over the years. And he took satisfaction in knowing it. He sighed heavily.

"What's the matter?" Tim asked quietly. "Feeling guilty?"

"Yes. I shouldn't have come tonight. Heather's been making noises lately—serious noises—about marriage."

"Does that surprise you?"

"No, not really."

"Have you made her any promises?"

"No."

"Then why do you feel guilty? Heather's a big girl. She knows how the game works." Tim winked at a pretty brunette who was giving him the eye from the other side of the crowded room.

"People had the right idea years ago," Nick said. "Marriages were arranged in a businesslike manner. In exchange for this, I'll give you this. No crazy ideas about spending every minute of your time together, sharing every thought." As Nick talked, he watched Heather, who was regaling a group of four other people with a long story they seemed to find hilarious. She certainly was beautiful. Tall, slender, curved in all the right places. She was smart enough, she was entertaining, she was passionate. But she was also possessive and demanding. She would smother him. He'd had that sort of relationship once. It hadn't worked then, when he was younger and more flexible. It certainly would never work now.

No, he was right to break off with her. Right to proceed with his plans. He did want to marry again because he wanted children and a normal home life. But this time, he'd find himself a wife using the same strategy and careful planning he used in all his successful ventures.

An image of the slim, graceful young woman he'd interviewed earlier in the day filled his mind. He saw her as she'd looked that morning—calm and lovely, with hair the color of sunlight and eyes the shade of frosted leaves—listening to his proposition. He remembered her quiet dignity and the sharp intelligence he'd seen in her eyes.

She hadn't believed him when he'd told her his reasons for wanting her to do the story on him. But after stating her legitimate reservations, she'd accepted the assignment. Once she realized he wouldn't change his mind, she had given him no further argument. That acceptance had pleased him, reinforcing his belief that Claire Kendrick was sensible and rational, someone who would listen to reason, someone who could be managed. If there was anything Nick hated, it was someone who didn't know when to concede or when to cut their losses. Someone who allowed their emotions to rule their actions instead of logic.

He smiled, filled with a sense of anticipation. He wondered if his other beliefs about her would prove to be true. Somehow, he thought they would. The next few weeks should prove to be very interesting. Very interesting, indeed.

TWO

Claire tightened her grip on her mother's hand as she swallowed against the lump in her throat. Kitty's eyes, the identical soft gray-green as her own, watched her intently.

"How are you feeling today, Mom?" Claire asked.

The expression in her mother's eyes remained the same: slightly quizzical as they stayed fastened on Claire's. Then she smiled—a slow, sweet smile. "Kitty's dress is pretty," she said. She lifted the skirt of the pink and white striped dress—a dress Claire remembered her mother buying at least ten years earlier—one hot summer day in August. Claire's father had accompanied "his two girls" on their shopping trip, and Claire could still see the pride reflected in his eyes as he studied his beautiful Kitty pirouetting in her new dress. A familiar sadness gripped Claire at the bittersweet memory. John Kendrick had loved his wife and daughter, but he hadn't been sensible enough to provide for them if anything ever happened to him.

Forcing her attention back to her mother, she said, "Yes, it's a pretty dress."

Kitty's smile remained, but her eyes drifted toward the doorway and the sound of laughing voices coming from the hall.

As she had a thousand times before, Claire wondered how much her mother comprehended. Sometimes when Claire talked to her, Kitty responded quickly, with an almost adult logic. Other times her responses were childlike, if she responded at all. On those days, Kitty's attention span, never very long, was almost nonexistent. The doctors had said there was so much damage to her brain that Kitty had the mentality of a two-year-old.

Claire used to think Kitty's condition was contradictory, because she had retained most of the natural, physical instincts of a woman, flirting outrageously with her doctors and acting the part of a coquette whenever any man was near. In the six years since her mother had been injured, Claire had seen Kitty pout coyly one minute and need help buttoning her sweater the next. One day, she could put makeup on unassisted—and she always wore makeup—the next she couldn't remember how to tie her shoes. But the doctors had assured Claire that this was normal in cases such as Kitty's.

After the boating accident that had killed her father and injured her mother, Claire had tried to keep Kitty at home with her. But it hadn't worked. Kitty would put water on to boil, then walk away and leave the kettle; she'd wander off if Claire wasn't looking, then Claire would spend frantic minutes driving up and down the streets looking for her. She'd cut herself trying to slice an apple or a piece of bread. She'd burn herself touching the hot electric coil of Claire's stove. She would walk outside in her underwear and think nothing of wandering through the house naked.

After only a few days of this behavior, Claire knew she'd have to do something. But what? If she tried to keep her mother with her, Kitty would require round the clock care—ideally a trained nurse to tend to her needs. Claire simply couldn't afford it. Although Pinehaven Nursing Home was very expensive, at-home individual care was more—much more. So Kitty had ended up at Pinehaven, and Claire had learned to live with her sorrow and guilt, which she assuaged by visiting her mother several times a week. And despite everything, Claire clung to the faint hope that someday, somehow, her mother might recover.

Now Kitty began to hum. Claire bit her bottom lip and stared out the window. The rain had continued unabated all day long. It was depressing—like my life, she thought—then immediately shook off the dreary thought. There was no percentage in feeling sorry for herself. Instead, Claire always tried to focus on her blessings. She had a good job, she was healthy and strong, and she had the support of her Aunt Susan and Uncle Dale as well as a few loyal friends.

I'll make it. I can make it.

All I have to do is take life one day at a time.

The one-day-at-a-time philosophy was one self-help groups taught, and it was a wise credo, Claire felt. There really wasn't any sense in worrying about the future because so much of Claire's future was beyond her control. Unlike other young women, she had stopped dreaming about marriage and children. Who would be willing to share the crushing financial and emotional burden Kitty's chronic condition had imposed?

Dreaming of any other kind of life would only make her own prospects seem more bleak, and Claire didn't want to become bitter—one of those people who resented their lot in life and took it out on everyone around them. No, much better to adopt a one-day-at-a-time outlook and concentrate her energies on moving up in her chosen career.

Thinking about her career caused her thoughts to meander back to the morning's interview with Nick Callahan. Once again, she realized this was a big chance for her—a chance to really solidify her niche in the company. And if a promotion, bringing more money, should result from it, her life would be eased considerably. Even a couple of hundred dollars a month more would make a tremendous difference in the quality of her life—and in what she was able to do for Kitty.

Sighing, she forced her attention back to her mother's dreamy face and soft contralto voice as she hummed some old song. "Yesterday." Her father's favorite song. Tears misted Claire's eyes as suddenly she was gripped by nostalgia. Yesterday. How many yesterdays had she come home from school and heard her mother singing in her clear, sweet voice? Those had been such carefree, happy days. She had always felt so secure. She had always known how much both of her parents loved her.

Other girls had complained bitterly about their mothers. How they didn't understand them. How mean they were. But Kitty had been a loving, supportive mother—someone Claire could always count on. Claire knew many of her friends were envious because she and Kitty were so close. *Oh, Mom. I miss you so much. I wish—*

"Claire?"

Claire looked around. She hurriedly composed herself, blinking away her tears when she saw her mother's doctor standing in the doorway to Kitty's room. Dr. Aaron Phillips had been overseeing her mother's care ever since Claire had put her into Pinehaven. His lined face was kindly, his dark eyes caring.

"How are you?" He flipped through her mother's chart.

"I'm okay. How's she doing?" Claire walked to where Kitty was sitting and smoothed a strand of gray-blonde hair back from her forehead. Kitty stopped humming, her eyes flicking from Dr. Phillips back to Claire.

"About the same. Aren't you, Kitty?" He smiled down at his patient, and Kitty preened, stretching like a cat.

Claire heard the absence of encouragement in his flat statement. She knew he really cared, that he sympathized with the plight of both of them, but he never held out false hope. He told Claire once that he considered it a criminal act to give people hope when no hope existed.

"Better to let them face the truth. Then they can get on with their lives, make plans," he said unequivocally. Normally Claire appreciated his candor, but occasionally she wished he'd give her a comforting platitude—something she could hang onto—something that might shore up her crumbling faith and natural optimism.

Twenty minutes later she brushed a light kiss against Kitty's soft cheek, turned on the television set, and said, "Good-bye, Mom. I'll see you soon."

" 'Bye," Kitty said distractedly, her eyes firmly fixed on the television screen.

To dispel her sudden sense of gloom, Claire whispered, "I love you." There was no answer from Kitty. Claire turned and walked out the door. She could hear Kitty laughing happily and clapping her hands at something she saw on television. Once again, Claire blinked back tears, this time angrily. What was wrong with her? It wasn't Kitty's fault she didn't care whether Claire stayed or not. A two-year-old couldn't be expected to understand the concept of someone else needing reassurance . . . or love. A two-year-old was totally wrapped up in her own world, and the only needs she understood were hers.

Face it! Yesterday will never be recaptured.

Claire sighed wearily. She was exhausted, and it was after nine. As she drove home through the rain, she couldn't help thinking how wonderful it would be to have someone to go home to. Someone who would understand her plight and who would share her burden. But what man in his right mind would want to be shackled by Claire's problems?

The next morning dawned bright and nearly cloudless—the front gone toward the Louisiana coast—and the air had an invigorating nip to it. On days like this, Claire's spirits always lifted. But by the time she reached her office, her good mood was tempered by a return of yesterday's anxiety. Just thinking about going up to the 50th floor at nine o'clock caused a knot to form in her breast, and by the time the hands of the clock showed five minutes to nine, her stomach was jumping.

She took several deep breaths as she rode up on the express elevator. It was ridiculous to be so nervous. Nick Callahan wouldn't bite her.

The elevator dinged its arrival. The doors slid open,

and as she stepped off onto thick gray carpeting, she forced herself to breathe evenly. She was proud of her easy smile and relaxed voice as she greeted Wanda.

"Mr. Callahan is expecting you, Miss Kendrick. He said for you to go right in." The secretary returned Claire's smile and gestured her in the direction of Nick Callahan's office, then returned to squinting at her computer terminal.

The heavy walnut doors stood open and bright sunlight poured through the plate glass windows. Claire could see the cathedral-like peaks of the NCNB Center building and the angled glass roofs of Pennzoil Place as she glanced at the view.

Nick Callahan rose to greet her, extending his tanned hand. She took his hand and clasped it firmly, looking him straight in the eye.

He returned her handshake and smiled briefly. If possible, his eyes looked even bluer this morning in the strong sunlight. Claire could feel herself responding to his compelling gaze. That, coupled with the aura of power he exuded, were enough to cause her pulse to flutter. No wonder he was such a respected and feared adversary.

"Good morning, Miss Kendrick."

"Good morning."

"Please have a seat." He waited until she'd taken one of the burgundy chairs, then sat in his own large, black leather one.

Claire withdrew a yellow pad and a fine-point felt-tipped pen from her briefcase.

"Before we start on the briefing, I'd like to ask a favor of you."

"All right." She opened the pen.

"When the two of us are in a business environment

with others, as we will be at this morning's managers' meeting, I think addressing each other as Mr. Callahan and Ms. Kendrick is necessary. But when it's just the two of us, could we drop the formality? I'd like you to call me Nick and I'd prefer to call you Claire.'' He smiled again, the same mocking smile he'd exhibited yesterday. Its effect on Claire was instantaneous. She felt exactly like she'd felt when she was fifteen years old and jumped off the ten-meter diving platform because of a dare.

"All right . . . Nick." Saying his name aloud gave her a funny feeling in the pit of her stomach. The smile played around his mouth as he watched her intently, almost as if he knew how uncomfortable and self-conscious she felt. She had a strong urge to smooth her hair, to touch her pearl earrings, to make sure there was no lipstick on her teeth. But she smothered it, sitting quietly as she waited for his next instruction.

She knew it wasn't a good idea to call him by his first name. The familiarity would change their relationship. Already, just saying his name once had broken down a barrier between them. Why had he suggested it?

He glanced away, picking up a paper from his desk, then he handed it to her. "That's the agenda for this morning's meeting—so you'll know what's going on. The following page is a list of the attendees. I had Wanda list their titles and give you a brief description of their function within the corporation."

"Thank you." Claire read through the agenda quickly, then turned to the list.

"Let's go through them together," Nick suggested. "The first name on the list is Paul Branch, Vice President of our Engineering Division. He's an old hand with the company, started with me when we had one job and no money to speak of. He's loyal and conservative."

Claire made a quick note next to Branch's name.

"Ben Bullard is Vice President of our Construction Division. He's only been with us for three years. He spent more than twenty years in Saudi Arabia and has excellent field experience. He's stubborn, but brilliant."

Claire scribbled another quick note.

"Next on the list is Hank Conti, Vice President of the Project Management division. Hank is a relative newcomer, been with us about two years after working all over the world. Then comes Albert Girard, Vice President of Finance. Have you met Bert?"

"Yes, briefly."

"He's our youngest vice president and very ambitious. I have a feeling he's angling for my job."

Claire looked up and Nick smiled briefly.

"Am I going too fast for you?" he asked.

"No."

"Any questions so far?"

"No." It was too soon for questions, she thought. So far, these men were only names on a sheet of paper.

Nick quickly went through the rest of the list, ending with Ken Boudreaux, Manager of Human Resources and Public Relations. Claire's department fell under Ken, so she knew him, although not well.

She noticed the absence of any female names and almost said something, then thought better of it. She was here to write an article, not to champion causes.

"Normally, Tim Sutherland would also be attending the meeting. He has a law background which serves us well. I depend upon him to advise me on all matters concerning contracts and administration." When she didn't answer, Nick shuffled through some other papers on his desk, selecting one and handing it to her. "That's my schedule for the rest of the week. From now on, Wanda and Tim will keep you up to date on any changes. They'll try to give you advance notice, especially if you're going to be required to leave Houston, but occasionally you'll be called at the last minute. My schedule is erratic at best."

Claire nodded. A shaft of sunlight slanted across Nick's desk and the gold watch at his wrist glinted. She could see fine dark hairs curling around the band. His wrist looked solid and strong.

The clock on his credenza chimed the quarter hour, breaking her thoughts.

"The meeting will start promptly at ten," he said. "It's going to be in the board room. Wanda usually puts coffee and sweet rolls out about now. Since we're finished, why don't you go on in and have some coffee and relax until the meeting starts?"

Claire put her pad and pen back in her briefcase. "All right, but what exactly do you want me to do during this meeting?"

"Watch, take notes, see if there's anything you can use for the article. Then, when the meeting's over, I'll take you to lunch and we'll talk."

The meeting went smoothly under Nick's guidance. He listened intently as each divisional manager gave a report on his department. Then current projects were discussed, centering on problems with the construction of a floating methanol plant and the bid on an offshore pipeline project. There was only one incident that marred the even flow, an incident that reinforced Claire's belief that Nick Callahan's surface charm and mild manner would disappear in seconds if his will was challenged. Bert Girard, the young financial vice president, disagreed with an expenditure Nick advocated. When Girard's opposition took the form of sarcasm, Nick's eyes narrowed and his voice hardened. "I don't need your approval, Bert. Shall we go on?"

The atmosphere was thick with tension for a few seconds, then Girard nodded, and the moment passed. Claire decided she wouldn't want to be on the receiving end of Nick's displeasure.

At eleven-thirty, Nick interrupted Hank Conti, who was listing the pros and cons of bidding on a new chemical plant project.

"I have a lunch reservation for noon, so I'd like to wrap this up fast. Can you sum up in five minutes, Hank?"

Ten minutes later, all but a few of the men had already left the conference room. Nick strode over to where Claire still sat. "Ready?" He smiled and his eyes were warmly admiring as he looked down at her.

Claire swallowed. She knew she should remain objective and businesslike with him, but she suspected his smile would be her undoing. Even though she knew the smile masked a tough will and determination to get his own way; even though she knew he used it to achieve his objectives and disarm his opponents; even though she knew he was deliberately turning on the charm; she could feel herself succumbing to its seductive appeal. Unfortunately, Nick Callahan and his dangerous smile made her all too aware of herself as a woman.

"Yes, I'm ready." She stood, picking up her briefcase and smoothing down her skirt.

"Let's go, then." He led the way to the elevator, and when it came a few minutes later, he waited for her to precede him. "I hate elevators," he confided with a self-deprecating smile. "I get claustrophobic in them."

It amazed Claire that the self-assured Nick Callahan—a man who instilled fear in other men—could himself be prey to such an ordinary fear. "Really?"

"Don't you believe me?"

"You seem like the type of person who isn't afraid of anything."

"I'm only human."

She smiled. "That's good to know. Can I put that in my article?"

"It's your article," he said. Just then the elevator doors opened noiselessly. Two laughing women entered and said, "Hello, Mr. Callahan."

"Hello, Renee . . . Shelley."

Claire saw the admiring glances the women gave him. No wonder they admired him. Most of the men Claire knew couldn't compare to Nick Callahan. And it wasn't just his polished looks or the way he dressed; his magnetism stemmed from his aura of importance and power. Very simply, he was a man you couldn't ignore.

The elevator doors glided open and he took her elbow, steering her through the throngs of lunch-goers in the lobby. Several men spoke to him as he and Claire made their way out the door and Nick responded pleasantly but didn't linger, even when one of them would have stopped him.

"Not now, Sandy," he said. "Call me later this afternoon."

As they emerged from the revolving doors into the bright January day, Claire took a deep breath. Today's weather was her favorite: clear, cold, and sunny. She didn't even mind the slight wind that whipped at her skirt, although she buttoned her jacket against the chill.

Nick took her arm once more as they descended the flat stone steps to the street level. It was only then that Claire noticed the black limousine waiting at the curb with a uniformed driver holding the rear door open.

Claire felt like Cinderella in her fairy-tale coach as she was assisted into the plush interior of the limousine. She nestled back into the plump cushions as Nick entered and sat beside her. She was so rarely pampered; she might as well make the most of this, she thought.

He turned to her. "Hungry?"

She nodded.

"Good." He leaned forward and spoke to the driver, who nodded and skillfully pulled away from the curb and into the stream of traffic on Louisiana Street.

Nick turned back to her, and Claire's heartbeat accelerated as his riveting blue eyes studied her. "So, what are yours?" he asked softly.

"What are mine?" What on earth was he talking about? She could see the smile lurking at the corners of his mouth and hovering in his eyes. Momentarily confused, Claire dropped her eyes. When she once again raised them, he chuckled, and her heart bounced at the warm, resonant sound. *Careful*, she cautioned herself. *This man is your boss. This is not a date.* But his nearness, and the warmth in his eyes, were impossible to resist. Betty had been right, Claire thought distractedly, as her pulse raced and her silly heart skipped under his flattering attention. He *does* positively ooze sex appeal.

"I told you my hang-up," he said. "I think it's only right you should tell me yours."

She forced herself to laugh and keep her voice

casual. "I'm the one who's supposed to be interviewing you, not vice versa."

"Humor me," he said.

Although his voice still held a teasing note, Claire knew he was serious. Suddenly, she was reminded of the wolf in "Red Riding Hood," and how he said, "The better to see you with, my dear." The sense of uneasiness that had been so strong yesterday came flooding back. This man was too slick, too accustomed to controlling and manipulating both people and events. And although she still wasn't quite sure what he wanted from her, she knew instinctively that she'd have to stay on her guard at all times. She would have to keep her head and her wits about her, which meant she'd better fight as hard as she could against the attraction she couldn't deny. An attraction that, if she gave in to it, could only mean trouble.

"Well, let's see," Claire said lightly. "I'm afraid of the dark; I always keep a night light on. I don't like driving at night—actually, I'm not fond of driving, period. I'm terrified of spiders and I get positively crazy when I see a cockroach. Other than that, I'm your normal, garden-variety coward."

"I don't believe that for a minute," he said.

Something in his tone alarmed her. For a minute she almost thought . . . no, that wasn't possible . . . no one at work knew her personal situation, not even Betty O'Neill. Claire had never said a word about Kitty to any of her co-workers. She knew her hope that Kitty's condition would change, that she would become the same woman she had been before the accident, was irrational, but still she hoped. Plus, she hadn't wanted people to feel sorry for her. Too much sympathy would be almost as bad as none.

Shaken, Claire looked out the window in an effort to gain her equilibrium. She was startled to see they were cruising up Memorial Drive, leaving the downtown skyline behind.

"Where are we going?" she asked, finally meeting his eyes again, feeling their force.

"To one of my favorite places."

Five minutes later the limousine swept into the curving driveway that was the entrance to the Rainbow Lodge. Claire had never been inside the restaurant, but she'd heard about it from Peachey, who had been wined and dined there often.

With a speed and personal attention that couldn't help but impress Claire, she and Nick were guided upstairs to a small, private dining room that held a fireplace with a cheerful blaze. Glass-paned doors led to a small balcony shaded by enormous oak trees. The table for two had been placed in front of the fireplace, and Claire sighed with pleasure as she looked around her. "This is a beautiful setting," she said.

"Yes," he agreed.

"It's like a piece of the 19th century in the middle of all the bustle and energy that's Houston," Claire said, noting the authentic furnishings and antiques.

After the waiter had taken their order, Nick said, "What did you think of the meeting?"

"I thought it was interesting. There were projects discussed that I didn't understand, though, and I'd like to ask you about them." She reached for the notebook in her briefcase.

He shook his head. "No business talk during lunch."

"But—"

"I mean it. Put that notebook away."

With a flash of irritation, Claire bent down and

stuffed the notebook back into her briefcase. How could she hope to do a thorough job when he seemed determined to inject a personal element? She couldn't. He would set the tone because he was her boss. Her determined, manipulative boss. Someone totally accustomed to getting his own way. Claire's sense of self-preservation kicked into overdrive.

"So, tell me what you do for fun," he said, leaning back in his chair as their waiter served them small Caesar salads.

"Mr. Callahan—"

"Nick." Amusement danced in his eyes like blue flames dancing in a gas fire.

Claire sighed. "Why do you want to know?"

"Over the years I've discovered it's useful to know everything there is to know about people—whether they're friends, employees, or adversaries. That way, I'm never surprised."

Although he said it lightly, Claire was sure he meant every word. "We're not here to talk about me," she said. "What do *you* do for fun?"

"I asked you first."

He wasn't going to give up. Resigned, she said, "Well, I read a lot."

"That's it? You can't read all the time." He buttered a piece of French bread and took a forkful of salad.

"I don't read all the time. There are lots of other things I like to do."

"Such as?"

Their conversation ceased as the waiter appeared to refill their water goblets. Then Nick said, "I'm still waiting. What else do you do besides read?"

For a minute Claire considered telling him it wasn't

any of his business. "I like to cook and I like gardening and I like to go to the movies."

"No physical exercise? How do you stay in such good shape?" His eyes boldly assessed her.

Mentally squirming, Claire said, "I walk every day and I roller skate."

"Roller skate!"

"Sure. What's wrong with that?"

"Nothing," he said as he reached for another piece of bread. "It's just that you don't look like the roller-skating type."

Claire couldn't help smiling, even though she was still irritated with him and with the entire conversation. "And what type is that?" She took a bite of her salad, savoring the crisp Romaine lettuce and the excellent dressing.

"Oh, you know," he said, "big and muscular and tough looking."

"You're talking roller derby, I'm talking roller skating at a neighborhood rink." Her smile expanded to a grin at the expression on his face. "It's fun. You should try it sometime. Inexpensive and great exercise."

"Okay," he said quickly. "You talked me into it. Let's go roller skating Saturday night."

Alarm streaked through her. Pretending he hadn't suggested the outing, she said, "Saturday night at the roller rink is kids' night." Then, quickly, before he could answer, she said, "It's your turn. What do *you* do for fun?"

He waited as the waiter cleared their empty salad plates, replacing them with their entrees. "I ski. Sky dive. Climb mountains. Fly."

Her heart beat with a slow thud as their eyes locked. "You like to live dangerously, in other words."

His mouth slowly curved into a full-of-the-devil smile. "I guess you're right." His eyes glinted as he watched her. "I also like to gamble."

Claire's pulse quickened at the undercurrents she sensed behind his casual admission. *Are you gambling now, Mr. Callahan? Gambling that you'll charm the socks off me—that this luxurious treatment and flattering attention will completely disarm me—so that whatever it is you really want from me will be yours for the taking?*

As if he'd read her mind, his face sobered, and his gleaming blue eyes pinned hers.

Claire stared back at him. Her mouth was dry with excitement. "Do you ever lose?"

"Not often," he said. "Not bloody often."

THREE

"The steaks are almost done," Peachey Hall said as she turned the two strip steaks under the broiler. "How's the salad coming?"

Claire looked over her shoulder at her friend and smiled. "It's ready."

"Good. I'm sure hungry."

"You're always hungry," Claire said. "And I don't know where you put it." She eyed Peachey's willowy figure.

"I put it here," Peachey said, grinning, as she patted her rear. "That's where black chicks always put it."

Claire rolled her eyes. "You're crazy. There's not an ounce of extra fat on you. Most women would kill for your figure." She leaned against the kitchen counter as Peachey languidly set the small round table in the corner of the kitchen. Every movement was graceful. Even if Claire hadn't known that Peachey was a top model, she would have guessed it from the way her friend moved, like a finely tuned instrument, all economy of motion, all fluid grace.

She was so beautiful, Claire thought. A show-stopper face, a tall, elegant body—what more could any woman ask for? In addition, her skin was gorgeous—a wonderful shade of milk chocolate—complemented by high cheekbones and slightly slanted eyes, a look that was enhanced by the sleek, shining head of black hair that Peachey normally wore pulled straight back from her face and twisted into a thick knot at the crown of her finely molded head.

As Peachey turned and met Claire's appraising eyes, she grinned and said, "What you lookin' at, girl?"

"I'm looking at you."

"Why? Did I suddenly sprout two heads?"

Claire laughed. "I *like* looking at you."

"Well, don't you be starin', white girl. You're makin' me nervous," Peachey drawled with an exaggerated accent.

"Knock it off, Hall. Don't start with the white girl routine, okay? I'm trying to conduct a serious conversation."

Peachey did an intricate jazz step, then leaned over to pull out the broiler pan and sniff at the two sizzling steaks. "Um um," she said, "don't they smell good? Hand me that platter, would you, Claire?"

Claire smiled and picked up the stoneware platter, handing it to Peachey who deftly transferred the aromatic steaks from the broiler to the platter. "I see the accent disappeared as soon as you started talking about the food," she said dryly.

"Food is serious business."

"This situation with Nick Callahan is serious business, too.'' Claire carried the salad bowl and rolls to the table.

Peachey stopped clowning. ''Sugar, I just don't see what you're so all fired up about.'' She offered the paper napkins and Claire took one. ''Unless there's something you haven't told me?''

Her mouth pursed thoughtfully as she studied Claire.

Claire's hands stilled over the salad bowl. For a moment she stared at Peachey. Then she took a deep breath, dumped salad into her salad bowl, and said, ''No, not really.'' She avoided Peachey's eyes as she poured Italian dressing over her salad.

''Hey,'' Peachey said. ''Turn those baby greens my way, girl.''

Claire looked up slowly.

Peachey's eyes gleamed brightly. ''You're hiding something.''

Claire shook her head. ''No, I'm not. It's just . . . well, I get the oddest feeling when I'm with him, Peachey. It's nothing you can put your finger on, but something about the way he looks at me really gets to me.'' Once more the image of the wolf and Red Riding Hood slid into her mind. She laughed self-consciously, knowing her words were going to sound melodramatic. ''He makes me feel as if he's the hunter and I'm the little baby deer.''

Peachey grinned. ''No wonder you're nervous.'' She spread her napkin over her lap. ''How old is this dude, anyway?''

Now Claire grinned. Dude. What would Nick think about being called a dude? ''He's forty-two, according to his official bio.'' Suddenly Claire felt better. Just having voiced her fear and having Peachey treat it seriously somehow diminished it in Claire's mind. ''I'm probably imagining the whole thing. He probably looks at everyone like he's considering adding them to his trophy collection.''

"Hm . . . I don't know. Most of the powerful men I've met don't automatically do that. They only act that way if they want something. If you have nothing to offer them, they simply look right through you. No, I think you're right. Your boss does want something from you . . . something more than a story. The question is, what?''

"My lily-white body?''

"Honey, if he wanted your lily-white body, I doubt he'd go through the elaborate build-up.''

"You're probably right.''

"Besides, a man like Nick Callahan can have all the lily-white bodies he wants.'' Peachey laughed.

Although Claire laughed, she knew Peachey's observation was close to the truth. The same thought had occurred to Claire more than once in the past two days. She was sure most women would knock each other down in their haste to offer Nick Callahan anything he wanted—in bed or out of bed. "Then what could he want? I've thought and thought, but I can't think of anything else.''

Peachey cut a piece of steak, then popped it into her mouth, chewing with gusto. She stabbed a forkful of salad and held it up, then said, "Maybe he's *really* interested in you. You know, seriously interested.'' She chewed slowly, watching Claire as she did.

Claire put down her fork. "That makes no sense.''

"Why not?''

"Because, as you said, he can have any woman he wants. Why would he be interested in me? I'm absolutely ordinary. In fact, I'm dull.''

Peachey frowned. "Claire, honey, I'm tired of hearing that bull. You are not ordinary. And you are not dull. So knock it off."

Claire smiled. "You're hardly objective."

Peachey looked exasperated. "Why are you putting yourself down? You're a beautiful woman. You're also smart, and when you're not feeling sorry for yourself, you can be a lot of fun. All in all, you're a pretty fabulous mega-babe."

Claire chuckled at the private pet name she and Peachey had adopted.

"And—" Peachey paused, amusement putting a twinkle in her eyes, "you are extremely fortunate to count another fabulous mega-babe as your best friend!" Grinning, she added, "So why wouldn't he want you? He'd be crazy not to."

Claire felt a rush of warmth. Peachey could always make her feel good about herself. "Thanks."

"Okay, we've settled that. But I do think you'd better be very careful around him, Claire. I've met a lot of men like Nick Callahan through my modeling, and I know the type. He's had a lot of experience with women. If he does have designs on you and your body, he'll know all the right buttons to push."

"Oh, I know that. I've already seen him in action. But I'm prepared, Peachey. He's not going to take me off guard."

"Don't be too sure."

Claire was almost sorry she'd told Peachey her misgivings. "I don't want you to worry about me. I'm probably imagining most of this." But remembering the disturbing glints in Nick Callahan's brilliant blue eyes, Claire knew she hadn't imagined anything.

"Maybe," Peachey conceded. "But don't forget

what I said. And watch your back. That's where surprise attacks come from.''

At 11:45 the next morning, Peachey's warning still lurked at the back of Claire's mind when Kim Michaels, the secretary Claire shared with Betty O'Neill, buzzed her on her intercom.

"Claire? Mr. Callahan is on line three for you," Kim said, excitement in her voice.

"Thank you, Kim," Claire answered calmly, ignoring the sudden fluttering in her stomach. She hadn't seen Nick this morning. He'd had a meeting with his lawyer, and he'd left word with his secretary that he'd call Claire when he returned to the building. She'd used the time by asking central files to send up any press clippings or articles they had concerning Nick or the company. She'd just finished reading the last article in the stack and felt much better equipped to ask some pertinent questions for the article she would write for *C.E.O.* She picked up line three.

"Claire Kendrick."

"Lunch will be ready in my private dining room in fifteen minutes."

Claire bit back a retort. What if she'd had plans for lunch? Was she supposed to devote every minute of her time to him?

"I hope you're hungry," he continued.

"As a matter-of-fact, I am." She heard the coolness in her voice and wondered if he would react.

"Well, why don't you come on up then?" He hung up, but not before she'd heard a chuckle. Half angry at his perfect self-assurance, half amused at her own reaction to him, she took out her compact to check her hair and lipstick.

Claire tried to ignore the butterflies in her stomach as she walked into Nick's office. It irritated her that she couldn't seem to relax in his company, that she always felt she had to be on guard, and Peachey's warning hadn't done anything to alleviate that feeling. In fact, now Claire felt more uneasy than ever.

Nick had been standing looking out the window with his back to the room, but he turned as she walked toward him.

The first thing she noticed was the admiring gleam in his eyes as his gaze raked her, taking in her simple black dress and teal jacket. "Let's go straight into the dining room," he said. Then he glanced down at her briefcase. "I see you came prepared to work." His eyes met hers, and for a moment she felt hypnotized by their brilliance. "I thought I told you no business during meals."

"If you needed me after lunch I didn't want to have to go back to my office," she explained, fighting to hold on to her irritation and against the pleasurable glow brought on by his admiring glance.

All during lunch, she had to keep fighting the urge to relax, to give in to the desire to simply enjoy this experience. She had to keep reminding herself that she was way out of her league with this man. But it was very hard because Nick seemed set upon charming her. The lunch was more the type of meal you'd order if you wanted to impress a woman and put her in a romantic mood. No ordinary chicken breast and salad for Nick Callahan. He'd ordered crepes filled with scallops and cheese accompanied by a romaine salad accented with mandarin oranges and almonds and dressed with a honey/poppyseed dressing. When dessert came, it was raspberry sorbet in a crisp, sugary tart.

All of this was accompanied by an excellent Reisling, which Claire declined.

"I get sleepy in the afternoon if I drink wine at lunch," she said.

"I insist." As he bent over to pour her wine, his fingers brushed her skin. The touch sent a dart of pleasure through her. His mouth curved into a lazy smile as he leaned back into his chair and lifted his wine glass in a silent toast.

He knows I'm nervous around him. To distract him and erase that knowing look, she said, "This is a lovely room." The dining room, adjacent to his office, was small and intimate, holding only one round table which would seat no more than six people. One wall was entirely made up of windows overlooking the downtown skyline, one wall held a beautiful fake fireplace, and the other two walls were adorned by two magnificent Monet paintings.

Claire couldn't help contrasting today's lunch with her usual lunchtime regimen of a tuna salad sandwich and an apple eaten sitting on the stone wall around the reflecting pool in front of city hall. What must it be like to live like this? she wondered. Able to conjure up anything you liked simply by asking for it.

For the rest of the afternoon, she kept a tight rein on her thoughts. She sat in his office, she asked questions, she made notes, she listened to his phone calls—which he unhesitatingly switched to the speaker so she could hear both sides of the call—and she was filled with reluctant respect for him by the time the afternoon ended. He was tough—the phone calls proved it—but he was also fair. And he listened. She'd been around some executives who just rolled right over people, never listening to what they had to say.

But Nick listened. He listened thoughtfully and quietly, interjecting a comment now and then. Once the other person finished with his point, Nick explained his position. It didn't surprise Claire that Nick's point usually swayed his caller to his way of thinking.

At five-thirty Nick said, "Let's call it a day."

Claire closed her notebook and picked up her briefcase. "What's on the agenda for the rest of the week?"

"Tomorrow I'll be tied up in meetings with customers all day, so you'll have a free day." Apparently noticing her puzzled look, he added, "I thought about having you sit in, but there's nothing to be gained by it. We're going to be discussing contractual differences—nothing I'd want in the article, anyway."

"Actually, that'll work out well. I need to sort through my notes and do an outline. I guess I'll see you on Monday then?"

"Sooner than that. Saturday night I'll be attending a reception at River Oaks Country Club in honor of the British consul general. I'd like you and Tim to accompany me."

Claire tried to hide her surprise. Although she should have, she hadn't realized he might want her company during the weekend.

If he had noticed her surprise, he didn't comment. "As far as I know, I won't need you on Sunday, though."

Claire's mind raced. What on earth could she wear Saturday night? "Is the reception formal?"

"Yes." He stood, and the afternoon sun slanting through the window lit his dark hair and bathed him with golden light. Claire thought he looked like a warrior prince, strong and invincible.

"Any other questions?" he said.

"No." Peachey would help her out. Although Peachey

was taller than Claire, they both wore a size six, and Peachey had dozens of dresses that were cocktail length. Maybe one of them would work. If not, Claire would think of something. She *did* have a long black velvet skirt. Maybe all she'd need from Peachey would be a good-looking top. And Peachey's fox jacket, Claire amended, thinking of her own five-year-old cloth coat.

"Then," he continued, walking around to the front of the desk so that they were only a few feet apart, "on Monday afternoon, I'll want you to fly to New Orleans with me. The company plane will leave from Hobby Airport at two o'clock. We'll come back on Wednesday."

As casually as she could, Claire said, "Will Tim Sutherland be going along?"

"Not this time."

Excitement and fear warred together in her mind. The prospect of spending two days with Nick in New Orleans couldn't help but excite her, but it was also a scary proposition. Peachey's warning echoed in her mind and Claire wondered what her friend would think about this trip.

On Saturday night as Nick pushed the button to the right of Claire's door, he wondered how she would act during the reception. So far, in all the time he'd spent with her, she'd been on her guard against him—hiding her feelings. Unless she blushed. He smiled, thinking of her blushes. They were charming, he'd decided. Charming and refreshing. She was the only adult woman he knew who actually blushed.

Her apartment complex was pleasant, he thought. Looking down at the tree-filled courtyard below and the orderly grounds, he decided it wasn't a bad place to live at all. Although the complex was small and located on a short, one-block street in far west Houston, his driver had had no trouble finding it.

Her door opened, and light spilled out behind her. His breath caught as he got a good look at her. She looked beautiful. She was wearing a long, black velvet skirt, and as she moved aside to allow him entry into the apartment, Nick saw that the right side of the skirt was slit up past her knee, allowing a glimpse of silk-stockinged leg. With the skirt, she wore a cream-colored lace blouse with a low, rounded neckline. Around her neck was a narrow velvet ribbon from which hung a small cameo. Her butter-yellow hair had been swept up, and Nick had a sudden urge to touch the little hollow at the back of her neck, to slide his fingers up under her hair and bury his face in her soft, scented skin.

His hands itched as she moved to pick up her coat from the back of a chair and he caught another peek of long leg. How could a woman look both cool and as sexy as hell? As he helped her into a short fox coat, he wondered how she had managed to buy it. With her financial burden there couldn't be anything left for luxuries.

He wondered what her reaction would be if she knew he was aware of her situation. He suspected she was proud, that she wouldn't like him knowing. He liked that. He was the same way.

Yes, he thought as he assisted Claire down the steep outside stairs toward the waiting limousine that looked so incongruous in the parking lot of the apartment complex, he was fairly certain he'd made the right choice with this woman, and the way things went in New Orleans should be the deciding factor.

*　　*　　*

The reception wasn't as bad as Claire had thought it would be. She'd expected to feel nervous, but her only nervous moment came when she was introduced to the British consul general and his wife. But once those few minutes passed, Claire actually started to enjoy herself.

The country club was magnificent, she thought, as she looked around at the sumptuous furnishings and the beautifully gowned and bejeweled women. The colors of their dresses were a feast for the eyes: vivid emerald and royal blue and purple and scarlet as well as black and white. The chandeliers glittered, the music was soft and tasteful, the laughter and conversation floated around her.

Nick seemed to know everyone, and Claire watched intently as he played the part of the perfect guest, complimenting each woman he talked with and sharing some anecdote or observation with the men. It amused her to watch him in action. He was like an actor with each movement or speech carefully rehearsed before it was shown to his audience. She wondered how he'd feel if she were to write that about him in the article. She suppressed a grin at the thought. He'd probably pin her with those bright, knowing eyes and tell her to get her Ph.D. if she wanted to practice the art of analysis.

Tim Sutherland interested her, too. Tonight he actually seemed human and, although he still wasn't exactly friendly, at least he wasn't throwing his usual verbal darts.

The only bad moment came after the three of them were at the reception for about an hour. A couple strolled up to Nick, and the woman—a beautiful redhead with a lush figure—said silkily, "Why, Nick! I didn't expect to see you here tonight. I thought you'd be too *busy.*"

Nick turned toward the couple. "Hello, Heather."
He nodded at her escort, a handsome, dark-haired man
with black eyes. "Armand." He turned back to the
woman. "Didn't you? I left a message for you with
your secretary."

"Did you?" Her tawny eyes blazed.

Claire could sense the tension in the air, and she
wondered who the woman was and what she meant to
Nick. An unexpected pang of envy pricked her.

Nick's smile was slow and knowing. "Loretta's not
up to her usual standards if she forgot to tell you."

The redhead gave her escort a secretive, full-of-
promise smile. "I *must* speak to her, then. An *important* message could go astray."

It was obvious to Claire, and she was sure to everyone else standing within earshot, what Heather was
inferring. Claire tensed, preparing for Nick's reaction
to the insult.

He surprised her. His only reaction was the widening
of his smile. His voice, which Claire was sure would
be full of biting sarcasm, was suspiciously husky, even
tender, as he said, "It was probably just a momentary
loss of efficiency. I wouldn't worry about it." Then
he leaned over and kissed the redhead's cheek, saying
affectionately. "You look absolutely gorgeous tonight,
Heather. Armand is a lucky man."

Claire saw the flush of surprise, then pleasure, then
something akin to pain, that flashed through Heather's
golden-brown eyes in rapid succession. Her own must
be full of admiration, she thought, as she realized just
how nice—no, *chivalrous*—his gesture and answer
really were.

He turned then, and introduced Claire, saying,
"Heather, Armand, I'd like you to meet Claire Ken-

drick. Claire, these are two old friends—Heather Richardson and Armand Fontayne.''

Heather had regained control of her emotions, Claire saw, and as the woman inclined her head, her expression was neutral, but Claire could see the question in her eyes as she studied Claire. Claire willed herself not to color under the redhead's scrutiny. *I'm not your rival*, she wanted to say. *I'm only an employee—no competition at all.*

"As usual, impeccable taste," Armand Fontayne said to Nick as he took Claire's hand. Then he bent and kissed it. Claire wanted to correct his assumption that she was Nick's date, but knew she would only call more attention to herself. Better to just let it pass.

After a few minutes the couple wandered off, and Tim turned to Nick. "I don't know how you do it," he said admiringly.

"Do what?" Nick said. He smiled at Claire and her heart gave a tiny leap of pleasure.

"Okay, play dumb." Tim pushed his hair out of his face and accepted an hors d'oeuvre from a passing waiter. "See if I care." Then he winked conspiratorially at Claire. "He thinks he's fooling us. He wants us to believe he has no heart at all—that he's completely ruthless and unfeeling."

"I *am* ruthless and unfeeling," Nick said, a crooked smile twisting his mouth. "Ask anyone."

"I give up," Tim said. "I'm going over there and talk to Beverly James. Let me know when you're ready to leave."

Later that night, as Claire thought over the evening, she acknowledged that Nick Callahan was a more complex man than she'd first imagined. More complex and devastatingly attractive. Unfortunately for her, she liked him a lot more than she'd thought she would. A lot more than was healthy or even wise. She'd feel much better about her situation if she'd never discovered he could be sensitive and generous in his dealings with people, that there was a warm inner person she might really enjoy knowing.

She remembered how she'd felt sitting beside him in the back seat of the limousine on the way to her apartment after the reception. The cocoon-like intimacy of the limousine, closed off from the driver, Beethoven's "Appassionata" floating around them, stirred feelings and desires Claire rarely acknowledged. Because she knew her needs would probably never be met, Claire had tried to bury her sensual nature, but there was some quality in Nick Callahan that brought all those feelings to the forefront of her mind as well as her body.

A deep shudder of longing shook her as she turned over restlessly in her bed and relived those long minutes when the two of them were enclosed in the warm darkness of the Lincoln, touching but not touching. Just like their lives. Touching, but not touching.

All day Sunday, Claire fought against thoughts of Nick. By the time she reached Pinehaven on Sunday night, she had finally managed to put him out of her mind. The visit with her mother depressed her, though. Tonight Claire was filled with a sense of futility and torn by her conflicting emotions: love, pity, sadness. She felt so impotent. She wanted so much for her mother and she was so powerless to give it to her.

She couldn't wait to leave, to get home to her apartment. No matter how small it was, she always felt a sense of peace once she shut the door against the world.

So, after helping Kitty with her dinner, Claire turned on the television set, then kissed Kitty's forehead.

"Good-bye, Claire," said her mother, eyes immediately turning toward the television screen.

"I won't see you again until Wednesday night, Mom. I'm going out of town on a business trip." Claire knew her mother didn't understand her most of the time and probably wouldn't care if she did, but Claire had fallen into the habit of telling Kitty about her life. In a strange way, Claire felt comforted by the act of confiding in Kitty. Just as she'd thought, Kitty didn't respond. Sighing, Claire picked up her purse and jacket.

As she turned to leave she saw Amy Provost, the head nurse on the night shift. Claire said, "Hi, stranger! It's good to have you back. Did you enjoy your time off?"

Amy's wide face broke into a grin. "Well, if you can call chasing after three grandchildren time off, I guess you could say I enjoyed it."

The two women talked for a few more minutes, then Amy's cheerful face sobered. "Claire," she said hesitantly, "have you gotten the letter about the raise in rates yet?"

Claire froze. "What raise in rates?"

Amy glanced over at Kitty, then said, "Why don't we go into my office and talk?"

Claire nodded. Her mind raced. Dear God, how could she handle a raise in rates? It was all she could do to pay the seven hundred dollars a month that was her share of Kitty's expenses; most months she could barely scrape it together. Even a modest rise in rates would throw the entire delicate balance of her budget into a tailspin.

Once settled in Amy's small office, Claire looked into the older woman's troubled eyes. "How much of a raise is it going to be?" Claire asked quietly, fighting against the panic that was threatening to push through the thin barrier of her self-control.

Amy hesitated, then said, "Three hundred dollars a month."

Shock rendered Claire incapable of speech. In her worst imaginings she couldn't have conjured a more disastrous development. What in God's name would she do?

"The powers-that-be say they have to do it," Amy was saying, her words barely penetrating the roaring in Claire's ears. "You should have heard the fight at the board table the day this was decided. Doc Phillips fought against it, but the directors were adamant. Seems we've been in the red the past nine months."

Claire barely heard her. Her thoughts whirled chaotically.

"I know what a shock this is to you. That's why I was hoping you'd come tonight. I think the patients' families will get the letters in the next day or so, and I didn't want you to read it without some warning." Amy sighed heavily. Her voice was gentle as she said, "Are you all right?"

Claire forced herself to answer calmly. "Yes. I'm fine."

"Are you sure? You look awfully pale to me."

Claire was far from fine and she knew Amy knew it. But Claire also knew she was teetering on the edge, and if she admitted how really terrified she was, she would fall apart, and she didn't want to do that here. She didn't want to do that to Amy.

"What about your aunt and uncle? Can they give you any more help?"

Claire struggled to focus her mind on Amy's question. "Aunt Susan and Uncle Dale are already helping

me all they can. And Uncle Dale is retiring at the end
of the year. I can't ask them for more.''

Claire knew her mother's sister and her husband
would have a drastically curtailed income when he
retired. She had been worrying about what she'd do if
they were no longer able to contribute the share they
now gave toward Kitty's care. With their contribution
and the portion paid by Medicaid, Claire had just been
able to meet the monthly payment to Pinehaven.

"There's always the state hospital,'' Amy said quietly.

"No!'' The word was like a gunshot in the room.
Claire clenched the armrests of her chair as she leaned
forward. "I can't put Kitty in the state hospital. Even
if I thought the facility was one she'd like, which I
don't, it's too far away. I'd be lucky to be able to visit
her once a month.''

"What will you do then?''

Claire swallowed. Tears burned her eyes, but she
blinked them away. Crying wouldn't do anyone any
good, least of all her mother. "I'll find a way.''

Amy sighed again. "If anyone can, you can.'' She
stood, then walked around her desk. She knelt in front
of Claire's chair and took Claire's chilled hands into
hers. Her voice was filled with sympathy as she said,
"But if you should change your mind . . . if you want
me to look into State for you, I will.''

The two women hugged.

Before Claire turned to leave, she said, "When do
the new rates go into effect? Do you know?''

"The first of March.''

Forty-five days. The words drummed through her
head. *Forty-five days*. She walked with unseeing eyes
out of Amy's office, out of the building, and out into
the cold, dark January night.

FOUR

Nick arrived at the Hedrick Beech hangar at 1:45 P.M. He'd left instructions for Claire to be brought to the airport for a two o'clock takeoff. She should be there soon. He felt a pleasant tingle of anticipation.

Dave Jennings, the company's senior pilot, was filling out the flight plan. He looked up as Nick approached, his lined face crinkling in a smile. "Afternoon, Mr. Callahan," he said.

"Good afternoon, Captain." Nick liked the older man. He had tried for years to get Jennings to call him by his first name, but the pilot wouldn't do it. Nevertheless, they had an easy camaraderie. The two of them had had many long conversations about Jennings's military career, in particular his days flying jets for the navy. Nick, who had been too young for Vietnam, had always wondered what it would be like to fly during combat.

"Gonna have a good day to fly. Weather's perfect." Jennings squinted against the bright January sun, his reflector sunglasses glittering half-ovals of opaque black glass.

Nick took a deep breath of the crisp air. There was a strong odor of oil mixed in with the fresh breeze. Jennings was right. The weather couldn't have been nicer. The sky was so blue it almost hurt his eyes to look at it and there were only a few wispy clouds scattered about. The Gulfstream jet they would be using today stood gleaming in the sunlight as a mechanic gave it a final check. The Callahan, International logo was a bright splash of purple and gold against its silver tail.

Nick loved planes. One of the greatest satisfactions his success had brought was the money to indulge this love. He only wished he could fly this one. So far, he was only licensed to fly propeller aircraft, but it wouldn't be long before he'd be ready to test out on turbine-powered planes. His instructor would probably sign him off now, Nick knew, but he wanted to accumulate his own personal goal of one thousand hours of instruction before going before the FAA.

The sound of an approaching car interrupted his thoughts and he turned. The limousine coasted to a noiseless stop about ten feet away. Gordon, his driver, climbed out, gave Nick a half salute, then turned and opened the rear door. That same tingle of anticipation pushed Nick forward as one slim leg, then another emerged from the car, followed by sunlit hair. Pleasure stirred deep within, surprising him by its unexpected strength. Smiling, he said, "Right on time."

She straightened and silvery green eyes met his. "Hello, Mr. Callahan," Claire said, sticking to the formal address they'd agreed upon in the company of others.

Nick immediately knew something was wrong. He could see it in her eyes, even as she made an attempt to smile brightly. But the effort fell far short of the genuine, warm smiles he'd already come to look forward to. Concern, immediate and strong, flooded him.

Gordon removed her bag from the trunk of the Lincoln and walked over to the waiting plane. Nick watched as the driver climbed up the portable steps and disappeared into the inside of the plane. Nick turned back to Claire. "Ready?"

She nodded but said nothing.

He stood at the foot of the portable steps and helped her up. His concern grew as he saw the dark smudges beneath her eyes and the weary slump to her shoulders. Yes, there was definitely something wrong.

Once inside, she made polite comments about the interior of the plane, which was devoid of the usual passenger seats and instead had been turned into one long, comfortable seating area with plush sofas, deep individual chairs with leg rests, and small conversational areas with tables, but he could see no real enthusiasm in her eyes. When he took her into the compact, fully-stocked galley, his particular pride, she said, "This is nicer than the kitchen in my apartment." But again there was no spark of real interest.

Nick sat opposite her, watched as she fastened her seat belt, then fastened his own. He picked up the hand microphone that connected him with the pilot's cabin. "We're ready, Captain," he said.

Within minutes the plane was accelerating down the runway and soon they were airborne and climbing. Claire stared out the window and Nick studied her profile. She looked tired and worried. "What's wrong, Claire?"

Her startled eyes met his. "Oh, I . . . I'm sorry. I was daydreaming," she said. "Did you say something?"

"I asked you what was wrong. Something's obviously troubling you." He kept his voice quiet and encouraging, the same tone he used when he was attempting to disarm a business opponent.

"There's nothing wrong," she said quickly. "I'm just tired. I didn't sleep well last night."

She was a rotten liar. He studied her faintly flushed face for a few moments, then said, "I'm glad that's all it is. But remember, if you *should* have a problem of some kind, I don't mind listening. I might even be able to help."

She nodded, giving him the first genuine smile of the day.

He smiled back. He wished she trusted him, but he guessed it was too early in their relationship for that. For the remainder of the flight they didn't talk. Claire leafed through the most recent issue of *Houston City* magazine or looked out the window, and Nick pretended to be engrossed in an article in *Engineering Monthly*. But occasionally he would steal a glance at her and each time he did, he would see the same troubled expression on her face.

Whatever was worrying her, it was serious.

Before the trip to New Orleans was over, he promised himself, he would find out what the problem was. He would also come to a final decision about her.

Claire walked into her suite at the French Quarter hotel where she and Nick were staying while in New Orleans. It was a beautifully appointed two-room suite filled with antiques. The bed was a four poster draped in pale peach satin and the bathroom was large and luxurious with all manner of amenities. Normally, she would have been thrilled to have the opportunity to stay somewhere like this. But nothing was normal today. For the past eighteen hours all she had been able to think about was the shattering news she'd received the night before.

Desultorily, she unpacked her clothes and put them away. What was she going to do? That one question had pounded relentlessly through her brain. But it didn't matter how many times she asked herself that question. There was no answer.

All last night, after Amy had given her the news of Pinehaven's rate increase, she'd gone over and over her options. Should she ask Peachey for help? Even though she knew Peachey would give her as much help as she could, Claire also knew she'd never ask. Should she go to Aunt Susan and Uncle Dale? They couldn't afford to do any more than they were already doing. A credit union loan? What would she use for collateral? And where was the money going to come from to pay the loan back?

Claire closed her eyes, resting her head against one of the bedposts. A dull headache throbbed at her temples.

The state hospital.

How could she?

What else could she do?

My whole life is falling apart.

Tears burned behind her eyelids, but Claire refused to give way to the temptation to cry. Crying solved nothing. She'd learned that long ago when she had first received the news of her father's death and her mother's prognosis. She'd cried buckets of tears, and in the end she was still faced with the same problems.

She massaged her temples wearily, then stood. She had to try to put this problem out of her mind. She didn't know what she was going to be expected to do here in New Orleans, but the worst possible thing she could do right now was not give her full attention to her job. More than ever, she must be an exemplary employee. Nothing must jeopardize her only source of income. Perhaps if she did an outstanding job on the article about Nick, she would get a raise.

Nick. He had been so sweet today, had seemed so genuinely concerned about her. For one instant there, when his blue eyes had captured hers with such sympathy, she'd been tempted to confide in him. The burden of her knowledge and fear had been so great, she had almost weakened. But she'd caught herself in time.

He was her boss. It was important to her future with Callahan, International that she keep their relationship businesslike and professional. If she told him her personal problems, her status would change in his eyes. Also, she didn't want him to pity her. She didn't want anyone to pity her. The only thing holding her together right now was her pride.

But it *was* considerate and kind of him to ask. She wondered if all the stories she'd heard about Nick were true. They must be true. No one attained the wealth and power he had without a strong streak of ruthlessness. But after that first stubborn insistence that she take the assignment, he'd been nothing but kind and considerate to her. And he'd also been very compassionate in the face of Heather Richardson's angry and rude remark Saturday night. She wondered which was the real Nick Callahan—the steely and determined power broker or the kind and sensitive man she'd glimpsed today. Perhaps he was both.

Thinking about Nick reminded her that she had four hours before they were supposed to meet for dinner. She may as well take advantage of the free time. She decided to take a long, hot bath filled with some of the scented bath salts she'd noticed earlier. Then she would put on one of those thick terrycloth robes provided by the hotel and rest until it was time to dress. She hadn't lied to Nick about that; she really hadn't gotten much sleep the night before. For the remainder of the trip she would try not to think about Kitty or money or anything except her current assignment.

When she returned to Houston was time enough to deal with everything else.

Nick worked in his suite until six. Then he shaved, took a quick, hot shower and, wrapped in the thick maroon robe provided by the hotel, poured himself a crystal tumbler of J&B. He sipped at the drink and gazed out the window at the busy street below. He was looking forward to the evening ahead. He hoped Claire was feeling better; he wanted her to enjoy herself tonight.

The minute he saw her walking toward him in the lobby of the hotel forty-five minutes later, he knew her spirits were greatly improved. She looked beautiful tonight, he thought. She was wearing a wool dress with a deep vee neckline and softly flaring skirt in a shade of dark forest green, the perfect complement to her fair hair and delicate complexion. Over her arm was the silver fox jacket she'd worn Saturday night. She'd done something different to her hair, too. It looked fuller and fluffier, framing her face like a golden cloud. She reminded him of pictures he'd seen of the young Grace Kelly, with her combination of classy elegance and hint of sexy mischief.

He saw the way eyes followed Claire's progress through the lobby and felt a surge of possessiveness. "You look lovely tonight," he said as he helped her with her coat. A light, flowery scent teased his senses. "Did you have a chance to rest?"

She smiled and he was gratified to see that the smile reached her eyes. "Yes, I did. And I feel much better for it."

"Good."

The cab ride to Antoine's was short, and they didn't talk on the way, but the silence wasn't unpleasant. Claire was not only beautiful, Nick decided, she was restful to be with. She didn't have that compulsion to chatter so many of the women he knew seemed to have.

Later, after they were seated in the restaurant and had placed their order, she gave him another smile. "This is my first visit to New Orleans," she said.

"Really? And you've lived in Houston all your life, haven't you?" He knew she had. He'd memorized her dossier.

"Yes, but somehow, although I always meant to come here, I never did."

"Well, we'll have to make sure we get some sight-seeing in then."

"Oh, don't worry about that," she said hurriedly. "We're here on business. I don't expect—"

"I know you don't expect it." He smiled. "Perhaps I'd enjoy showing you the city. I haven't acted like a tourist in years. It might be a nice change."

"Just what *are* we going to do here?"

"I have a number of meetings scheduled and I

thought it might be informative for you to attend them with me," he said smoothly.

"Oh, all right."

Their salads came and Nick was pleased to see she didn't pick at her food, but ate it with obvious enjoyment. For the rest of their meal he worked hard at keeping that relaxed look on her face and felt he was succeeding. He even had her laughing at one point.

Over dessert, she said, "Did you grow up in Houston?"

"No. I'm from Boston."

Her eyes widened in surprise. "Really? You don't have an accent."

He smiled. "I worked hard to lose it."

"Why?"

"Because when in Texas . . . at least that's my philosophy."

"How old were you when you moved to Houston?"

"Fifteen."

"Were your parents transferred here?"

"Something like that." Like an ever-changing kaleidoscope, memories of several sets of foster parents clicked through his mind. He never talked about his childhood. He rarely ever thought about those years. The memories were too painful and they served no purpose. But maybe later, when they knew each other better, he would tell her the truth.

The rest of the evening passed quickly. Too quickly, Nick thought. He enjoyed Claire's company. She was delightful to look at, intelligent to talk to, and charming. To extend the time before he had to take her back to the hotel, he suggested they go to the Café du Monde for coffee and beignets.

"Even though I've never been to New Orleans

before," she said, laughing, "I *do* know what beignets are and I can't handle another dessert tonight."

"Well, you can just have coffee and *I'll* have beignets," he insisted. "Come on," he added, "everyone who visits New Orleans has to go to the Café du Monde at least once, and preferably several times." He hailed one of the horse-drawn buggies. "And we're going in style."

Her eyes glowed with pleasure as he helped her into the buggy and they began the slow ride through the Quarter toward Jackson Square. Nick enjoyed watching her face as she took everything in: the narrow, cobbled streets; the throngs of people on the sidewalks; the lights and gaiety of the fabled neighborhood; the wrought-iron grillwork on the balconies of the buildings; and all around them the sounds of music and the clip-clop of the horse's hooves.

"This coffee is wonderful," she said later as they sat at one of the small tables in the covered patio.

"Aren't you glad I made you come?"

She smiled. "Yes."

Too soon it was time to go. Within minutes they were back at their hotel, walking through the lobby, riding up in the elevator. Claire's suite was on the fourth floor and Nick's was on the fifth, but he exited with her. "I'll just see you to your door."

"Well . . ." She turned to face him outside her door. "Thank you for a lovely evening. I enjoyed it more than I can say."

He studied her upturned face: the barest trace of pink on her cheeks, the soft gray shadowing her eyelids, the halo of silky hair surrounding her face, the rosy lips tipped into a sweet smile. His heartbeat quickened as their eyes met. Very slowly, her smile faded, and he sensed the acceleration in her breathing. The moment of awareness stretched, and he wondered if the expression in his eyes had given away his desire to kiss her.

No, he told himself. *It would be a grave tactical error to give in to this urge.*

"Good-night, Claire," he said softly, taking her hands in his and pressing gently. "I enjoyed it, too." He let go of her hands and backed up a step. "Pamper yourself in the morning. Order a room-service breakfast."

"Okay." The pink on her cheeks had deepened and her eyes held a faint trace of bewilderment.

"Let's plan to meet downstairs in the lobby at eight-thirty. My first meeting is at nine."

Deep in thought, he walked slowly back to the elevator.

The meetings had been interesting but tiring, Claire decided late the next afternoon, but they had certainly accomplished one goal: she hadn't thought about her problem all day. Now that she was back in her suite at the hotel, though, her mind inevitably turned to Kitty. She decided to call Pinehaven and check on her mother.

After calling and being assured that Kitty was doing fine, Claire once more prepared for an evening with Nick. She decided the black wool suit she'd worn that day would have to do. She'd only brought one dress and she'd already worn it once. She could, however, change into a dressier top. So, instead of the plain white crepe blouse she'd worn earlier, she donned a pale blue sweater trimmed in tiny pearls.

She grinned wryly as she looked at herself in the cheval-glass mirror. So far, she'd been on this assignment for less than a week and already she'd worn just about everything in her wardrobe at least once. Claire loved clothes and she wished she had a larger selection, but she'd learned she was better off to buy fewer but more expensive, well-made garments. They looked better and lasted longer, and in the business world they made a statement about the kind of person you were.

A snob, that's what, she told herself, but knew down deep that wasn't true. If she had a real choice, she'd wear blue jeans and T-shirts or sweatshirts every day of the week, with only an occasional pretty dress thrown in as a special treat.

Nick was taking her to Commander's Palace for dinner, he'd said, and Claire had read up on the famous restaurant. She was looking forward to eating there; eating out was an indulgence she could rarely afford.

Once again, the evening was perfect. Claire loved the restaurant, especially the view of the Garden District through the plate-glass windows, and Nick was the perfect host. He looked great, as usual, in his dark pin-striped suit and beautiful shirt. Claire noticed how the eyes of the women followed him as they moved through the diners to their table. No wonder. He was a man any woman would enjoy being seen with. And he was her escort.

The only incident marring the evening came about halfway through their dinner when a well-dressed couple who looked to be in their late thirties entered the restaurant with an older woman in a wheelchair. The man pushed the wheelchair, and his wife, who Claire decided was the woman's daughter, led the way to their table. They were seated only a few tables away, in a perfect position for Claire to watch them, and when she saw how solicitious the man was both to his wife and the older woman, Claire had to swallow against the lump in her throat. She had a sudden, vivid picture of what it might be like to have someone like this man in her life who cared not only for her but for Kitty—someone she could lean on during the bad times.

Bad times like now.

After that incident, Claire's spirits drooped and no matter how hard she tried to be a charming dinner companion, she knew she wasn't doing a very good job of it. She was sure of it when, after dinner, Nick said, "I think I'd better get you back to the hotel. You look tired."

"No, I'm fine, really." *Oh, dear, he must think I am a real dud. An ungrateful dud. Here I am, in one of the best restaurants in New Orleans, and I am gloomy and boring company.*

But Nick paid no attention to her protestations and hustled her into a cab and back to the hotel in record time. As they rode up in the elevator, he said, "Claire, would you mind coming up to my suite for a while? I'll order coffee. There's something I'd like to discuss with you."

Although alarm bells went off in her mind at the idea of going into his suite, Claire didn't know how she could refuse. She took a deep breath. "All right."

Don't be nervous, she told herself as he unlocked the door to his suite. And her nerves did settle down a bit as he quickly walked to the open door leading into the bedroom and shut it. He motioned her toward the dark blue Victorian sofa. She sat and waited while he called room service.

It didn't surprise her that their coffee arrived within ten minutes. Claire already knew people jumped when Nick so much as looked their way. She picked up her cup, her eyes meeting his as she sipped. The intensity of his expression caused her insides to begin fluttering once more.

"Claire, I wish you'd tell me what's wrong. I sense something troubling you and I'd really like to know what it is."

An image of the woman in the wheelchair flitted through her mind. Kitty's face, so innocent, so blank, superceded it. Suddenly, Claire's hands were trembling and the cup rattled against the saucer. She bit her bottom lip. *Pull yourself together!* She carefully laid the cup and saucer on the coffee table and held her hands together in her lap to keep them from shaking.

He was sitting opposite her and he leaned forward, his eyes twin pinpoints of blue. "Come on. Tell me."

She wanted to. The desire to unburden herself was so strong it was almost a physical pain.

He stood and moved around the table to sit beside her. He reached for her hands. The feel of his strong, firm hands closing around hers was her undoing. Appalled, Claire could feel tears sliding out of her eyes and down her cheeks. She yanked her hands out of his grasp and angrily knuckled away the tears. She started to stand. She had to get away. She was falling apart and she didn't want him as a witness.

"Claire, please . . ." He stood, too, putting his hands on her upper arms, and through the wool fabric of her suit jacket she could feel their heat. "Claire, look at me."

She slowly raised her head.

"Is it your mother?"

Shock reverberated through her. How did he know about her mother? *What* did he know about her mother?

"Yes," he said softly, "I know. I know everything about you." Before the import of those words had had a chance to sink in, he added, "Whatever it is that's worrying you, we can take care of it. But unless I know what it is, I can't do anything."

"You can't do anything, anyway."

"Try me."

She sighed. His surprising statement about her mother had accomplished one thing. Her urge to cry had disappeared. Now all she felt was a bone-numbing weariness. "Look, Nick, I really appreciate your concern, but this is my problem. I have to find a way to deal with it."

"It's not wrong to ask for help if you need it, Claire. The company helps employees deal with problems all the time. You know that."

She did know it. She also knew the company couldn't solve this problem.

"Can't you trust me enough to at least tell me what it is?"

She sighed again. Inching away from him, she sat back down on the sofa and, after a minute, he did, too. He didn't touch her and for that she was grateful. "It's really very simple. Since you know about my mother, you know I have her in a private nursing facility. It's very expensive and I've barely been able to make ends meet for a long time. Any unexpected expense is enough to send my budget into a tailspin."

He said nothing, but his eyes encouraged her.

"Sunday night I found out the nursing home is raising their rates. Raising them considerably. There's no way I can continue to keep my mother there. And I've been sick with worry ever since." She met his gaze.

"I see." For a long moment, he studied her, and Claire felt an unsettling flicker of fear at the unfathomable expression in his riveting eyes. "Well, I believe I have the solution to your problem."

Claire, mesmerized by his unnerving gaze, said nothing. The silence in the room settled around them like a velvet cloak.

Then he smiled and Claire's heart skipped a beat. "All you have to do is marry me."

FIVE

"Marry you!" Claire couldn't believe she'd heard him correctly. She stared at him. "We hardly know each other!"

"I know everything I need to know about you," he said quietly. His eyes looked like royal blue velvet, deep and dark.

"B—but, we don't . . . we haven't . . ." At a complete loss, Claire sank back against the arm of the couch. All thoughts of her problem had been driven from her mind by Nick's startling statement. "I . . . I don't understand." Why did he want to marry her? He'd never even tried to kiss her. Although the night before outside the door to her suite, she'd had a feeling he wanted to. And she'd be lying to herself if she didn't admit that the idea had been very appealing.

And, if she were going to be completely honest with herself, there *had* been other moments, too. Riding next to him in the limousine the day he took her to the Rainbow Lodge. Riding home with him the night they went to the reception at the country club.

But she'd certainly never expected anything like this. Last night during dinner she'd caught a speculative, almost predatory look in his eyes several times as he watched her across the table. Had he been thinking about this, even then?

"Look, Claire, I realize my proposal is probably a shock to you. I know that we don't have the kind of relationship people usually have when they contemplate marriage. But I've given this matter a lot of thought. I think when you've heard what I have to say, you'll see how sensible my proposition is."

Sensible. Proposition. Claire wasn't sure she liked the sound of those words. She still couldn't believe he was serious, although he certainly seemed so.

Apparently he took her silence for agreement because he continued smoothly, his expression solemn. "Half of today's marriages end up in the divorce court. And of the other half, fifty percent are unhappy after the first year. The only thing most couples have going for them when they marry is sexual attraction. They tell themselves they are in love, when what they really mean is their hormones are acting up."

Even if Claire had wanted to say something, his dogmatic statement would have silenced her. All cold facts, she thought.

"My first marriage was based upon the feelings I've just described. Jill and I had nothing in common, certainly nothing upon which to base a long-term relationship. We didn't even like each other very much. After we'd only been married a few months, I realized Jill expected a life of constant excitement, travel, parties. That sort of life is anathema to me. I do enough traveling for business and, although I have many leisure time interests, none of them appealed to Jill."

He grimaced. "I blame myself for the failure of the marriage. Jill never pretended to be different. I was the one who lied to myself. I thought once we were married, she'd be content to settle down, make a home, have children." He looked at Claire, but she couldn't think of anything to say.

Sighing, he continued. "Above all else, I wanted a quiet, peaceful home life. While we were dating, I enjoyed showing Jill off, taking her a lot of places. I guess she thought that's what our life would be like." He grimaced again. "And why shouldn't she? I never gave her any reason to believe otherwise. So after we were married, and I got tired of running around every night, she was very unhappy. She needed constant attention. And when she didn't get it from me, she began to look for it in other men. It got so that I was afraid to pick up a newspaper for fear of what I'd read about my own wife."

His jaw hardened. "I can't live that way. I *won't* live that way. I made up my mind when I married again, I would pick a wife with my brains instead of my . . . emotions." He smiled sardonically. "That's where you come in."

Claire felt shell-shocked.

"I want children and a peaceful, well-ordered home," he continued. "And I also want the freedom to come and go as I please—to attend to my business and other interests. Just for example, I go mountain climbing several times a year. I go with a group of men with similar interests. I have no desire to cart a wife along with me, nor do I want a big scene each time I prepare for a trip. I cannot stand scenes. Crying and shouting leave me cold. I won't put up with a petted, spoiled woman who will demand all of my time and attention. I want someone intelligent and reasonable, someone who will fit into my life but won't expect to take it over. I want a woman capable of developing her own interests—interests suitable and appropriate to her position as my wife. A woman who is willing to make a businesslike arrangement with me, someone who can approach marriage in a calm, sensible manner. I think you are such a woman.''

"A businesslike arrangement . . ." Claire echoed. She wasn't sure if she should laugh or cry. He sounded as if he were coldly placing an order for a luxury automobile instead of listing what he would or would not put up with in a wife.

"Yes. And why not? What's wrong with treating marriage as you would any other important contract?"

Claire stared at him. He was serious. He really didn't see anything wrong with what he was proposing.

"Now, I haven't gotten to this place in my life without knowing that any bargain, to be successful, must answer the needs of both parties.''

He smiled again, supremely confident, Claire thought, as she began to feel the first stirrings of anger.

"You need someone to provide financial security for your mother. I can certainly do that, and more. I am willing to sign legal documents that will protect both you and your mother for the rest of your lives. You will never have to worry again. In addition, you will also have a beautiful home, a generous personal allowance, the freedom to pursue your own interests, as long as they are suitable, and as much help as you want.''

He looked very pleased with himself. "This arrangement should work out extremely well for both of us.''

"And love? What about love?"

"Love fades. Respect and honesty don't. And in

addition to my respect and honesty, I can offer you comfort, security, and children.''

''I see.'' How could he be so impersonal? So unemotional? So sure she'd go along with this ridiculous idea? Her face must have betrayed her growing anger because all at once he hesitated, and a flash of uncertainty appeared in his eyes.

''I know you're probably shocked by what I've said,'' he said softly. ''After all, I've had weeks to think about it and you've only had minutes.''

Weeks? Had he been thinking of making this offer even before she'd started work on the magazine article?

''I don't want you to think that material things are all I'm offering you, Claire. Even though I don't believe in love, I admire you tremendously. You have strength and courage and character. You're also lovely and charming. I enjoy being with you. In fact, you have all the qualities any man would want in a wife and future mother of his children. If you agree to marry me, I promise you I will be a considerate, agreeable, and faithful husband.'' Then he smiled again, his darkly dangerous smile, the one that frightened her even as it fascinated her. ''You won't be sorry. I promise you that.''

But what would happen if either one of them should happen to fall in love with someone else? Claire wondered. *What happens if I fall in love with him*? She hurriedly shook off the thought. She had no intention of marrying him, so the question was moot. ''Tell me something, Nick,'' she said, ''you mentioned that you'd had weeks to think about this. How could that be? You only told me about the magazine assignment a week ago.''

He hesitated, then said, "The magazine assignment was a device."

"A device! What do you mean?"

"I mean," he interrupted smoothly, "that I wanted to spend time with you and I didn't want to raise anyone's suspicions—not yours, and certainly not any of my other employees. I had to think of a way I could do that and the assignment was what I came up with."

Claire jumped to her feet. "I don't believe this. I simply don't believe it! You lied to me! Not five minutes ago you were offering me honesty, and all this time you've been lying to me!" She knew her face was red, but she didn't care. She was suddenly so furious she felt like slapping him. She felt like a fool. Now everything made sense. No wonder she'd had misgivings from the very first. She'd been right to question his motives. But she'd never dreamed of anything like this.

He stood, too. "I'm sorry you're angry. I really don't blame you, but you have to understand how difficult it is for someone in my position. If I so much as look at a woman, the gossip columnists have a field day. I didn't want that to happen, mainly for your sake. I couldn't be sure this would work out and if I dated you in the ordinary way, then suddenly stopped seeing you, I knew it would put you in an awkward position, both personally and professionally. I didn't think that would be fair to you."

"Fair to me! You think lying was fair to me?"

"It was the lesser of two evils."

He refused to admit he was in the wrong. She couldn't believe it. The whole time she'd been diligently working and trying to come up with an original idea for the article, he'd been examining her much as he would a piece of horseflesh. Why, the whole thing was degrading. Disgusting. Not only had she been professionally duped, he now thought he could buy her. He had insulted every aspect of her as a woman and as a professional, and he didn't even realize he'd done anything wrong. The man was an insensitive clod.

She gritted her teeth and glared at him. "Well, it's too bad you wasted so much time because I'm not the least bit interested in your *proposition*. I'm not for sale!"

"Claire, please—"

"Forget it, Mr. Callahan. You'll have to buy a wife somewhere else." She whirled around and stalked toward the door.

"Think about it, Claire," he called after her. "After you've had a chance to calm down—"

Furious, she yanked open the door and flung herself out, slamming it behind her, cutting off his sentence. She marched down the hall toward the elevators, seething inside. Oh. If she wasn't a lady she'd . . . she'd . . . she'd kick him!

She punched the down button. Her heart was pounding so hard she thought it might burst right out of her chest. She was so furious. She felt so stupid, so gullible. What a conceited, arrogant . . . she couldn't think of enough names to call him.

Her fury lasted until she reached the safety of her suite. Then suddenly, like air whooshing out of a balloon, it was gone, and she felt hurt and confused. Tears burned behind her eyelids—tears because for one, stupid moment she'd almost believed that Nick was as attracted to her as she was to him.

Oh, you're such a fool. Too tired to fight her feelings

any longer, she threw herself across the bed and gave way to her tears.

Nick stared out the sitting room window. His view was the intersection of two of the busiest streets in the Quarter, but he hardly noticed them.

Had he made a mistake in being so blunt with Claire? Should he have eased into his proposition gently, given her more time, pretended a romantic involvement? Why did women, no matter how sensible they seemed, always want romance? Didn't they realize that romance belonged in books and movies and songs, but not in real life?

No, he'd been right to be honest. It was bad enough he'd lied to her about the magazine article. He'd always intended to be straight with her about his marriage proposition. Knowing where they both stood was the only way a marriage between them could work anyway, because he meant every word he'd said about the kind he wanted. It would have been stupid to lead Claire to believe he was in love with her because he wasn't, and he would never allow himself to be. Falling in love would negate his edge. And if there was anything he'd learned in the past twenty-odd years, it was the cardinal rule of business: You never allowed your edge to be weakened by personal emotions. His one failure in life—his marriage—had been directly attributable to his forgetting that rule.

So, he had done the right thing by telling Claire the truth. Still . . . he wished she hadn't been so upset when she'd left the suite. He hated thinking he was the cause of adding more stress to her life. Surely, after she calmed down, she'd begin to see the sound reasoning of his proposal, the benefits to both of them. He hoped by tomorrow morning, when they were scheduled to leave for Houston, she'd be ready to talk to him again.

But the next morning, when they met downstairs as arranged, he knew his hope was in vain.

"Good morning," he said. "The limousine is here. Are your bags on the way down?"

She nodded, her green eyes frosty.

He studied her. She looked beautiful, as always, but she also looked as if she hadn't slept well the previous night. Once again, there were shadows under her eyes, and Nick felt a twinge of conscience. She also looked remote. She'd twisted her hair into a severe chignon and her mouth was set in a determined line.

During the ride from the hotel to the airport, she kept her eyes straight ahead or she looked out her window. Not once did she glance his way, and Nick, although he still felt guilty about adding to her worries, began to be amused. It wasn't often that anyone ignored him. He wondered how long she'd keep it up.

When they were on board the company plane and she was settled into her seat, he said, "Would you like some coffee?"

She unbuckled her seatbelt.

"I'll get it," he said.

"Thank you." Her eyes were green ice. "I prefer to get my own."

Nick's amusement grew as she studiously ignored him throughout the entire trip. Even her body language was aloof. She sat upright in her seat, with her chin raised and her face turned away from him. He felt a surge of admiration for her. She was a woman of principle and she was not afraid of him. He was even more convinced he'd made the right choice with her.

But how was he going to convince her?

*   *   *

Claire knew he was watching her. A couple of times she was tempted to look at him, but she forced herself not to. Finally, though, she couldn't resist taking one peek. As luck would have it, he was looking at her but the look in his eyes confused her. She had expected to see that same confidence he'd displayed the night before, or perhaps even irritation or anger. Instead, his blue eyes had been filled with an uncomfortable warmth and unmistakable admiration. Claire hurriedly looked away. But her awareness of him intensified and she couldn't wait for the flight to be over.

Finally, they reached Houston. Gordon and the limousine were waiting, and now all Claire had to endure was the twenty-minute ride to the office. She was acutely aware of Nick seated beside her in the back seat of the limo. But, thank goodness, he didn't make any attempt at conversation. Claire knew she couldn't refuse to answer him if he talked to her, not if she hoped to keep her job, anyway. So, she was reluctantly grateful to him for his consideration of her feelings.

When the limousine pulled up in front of their building, Gordon was the one to help her out and she smiled warmly at him.

"You want me to put your bag in your car, Miss Kendrick?" Gordon asked.

"Thank you, Gordon. That would be a big help." She dug into her purse and fished out her keys, handing them to him. Then she walked toward the building.

"Claire, wait a minute."

She stopped but she didn't turn around. In a moment, Nick was at her side. She looked straight ahead. Several pedestrians cut a swath around them.

"Let's move off the sidewalk," Nick said. He took

her elbow and she allowed him to lead her up the stone steps. They stopped at the top.

Claire couldn't keep staring over his shoulder. She finally looked up. He smiled and her heart flip-flopped.

"Did you think about what I said?" His voice was low, intimate. His eyes were sparkling ocean-blue in the bright sunlight.

"Yes, I thought about it. My answer is still no." She raised her chin. "And no matter how many times you ask me, it won't change."

He smiled again and his eyes danced with amusement. "There's nothing I like better than a challenge, you know."

Claire swallowed. Something was jumping around in her stomach.

"The more stubborn an adversary, the more determined I am to win," he continued softly.

"You're very sure of yourself, aren't you? You really think I'm going to jump just because you whistled."

Their eyes locked.

"I'm sure of myself when I know I'm right."

"You're not right about this."

"We'll see."

Oh, he was infuriating. Claire wished she could think of something really snappy to say. A perfect put-down. Unfortunately, everything she thought of would make her sound juvenile. Knowing it was inadequate, she said, "Don't hold your breath." Then she brushed past him, pushed herself through the revolving door, and walked to her bank of elevators without looking back.

"Claire, if you're going to apply to State, you'd better get your application in. There's a waiting list," Amy warned.

It was two days after Claire's return to Houston—a Friday night—and she was standing outside the door to her mother's room while she talked with Amy Provost about her problem. "I just can't let my mother go to State, Amy."

"But what else can you do?"

Claire leaned her head against the wall. "I don't know," she said hopelessly. The trouble was, she had no choices. Nothing had changed. She still couldn't see any way out of her dilemma. *There's a way out. You just don't want to take it*, her inner voice chided. She shook the thought out of her mind. She would not marry Nick Callahan simply to insure her mother's future. She couldn't.

All the way home, her thoughts churned. She didn't sleep well that night. The next morning, in an effort to forget her problems for at least a little while, she decided to take a long walk. The weather looked beautiful—another clear, cold day. She put on a pair of sweats and her Reeboks, tied her hair back in a ponytail, and found her earmuffs. Just as she was about to leave the apartment, the telephone rang.

Claire didn't own an answering machine. It wasn't a necessity, so she couldn't justify spending the money. She thought about ignoring the insistent ring, but couldn't. What if it were something important?

"Hello?" she said.

"Claire?"

She'd have recognized his voice anywhere. "Hello, Nick," she said coolly. She ignored the thump, thump, thump of her foolish heart.

"Is this a bad time to call?"

"Yes, it is. I was just on my way out the door."

"Well, in that case, I won't keep you long. I just

wondered if you'd like to accompany me to the symphony tonight. It's an all-Mozart program called 'Mostly Mozart.' Do you like Mozart?" ·

Claire loved Mozart. And symphony tickets weren't necessities either. "Thank you, but I don't think so," she said.

"That's too bad. I thought after the symphony we might have a late supper at Harry's Kenya. But if you can't—"

"I didn't say I couldn't. I said I didn't think so."

He chuckled. "Still mad, I see."

"I'm not mad," she said, getting madder by the minute. He certainly could use knocking down a peg or two. But the warm, resonant sound of the chuckle sent quicksilver through her veins and caused her pulse rate to accelerate.

"Well, maybe another time."

"Look, Nick—"

"I guess I'll see you Monday, then. Good-bye, Claire."

For a long time after he'd hung up, Claire stood looking at the receiver in her hand. Nick had obviously meant it when he'd told her he loved a challenge. He hadn't seemed the least bit perturbed by her refusal today. If anything, he'd seemed amused. And, darn it, she'd *wanted* to go.

As she let herself out of the apartment and ran lightly down the steps, she had a feeling she was going to need all her willpower and self-control in the days ahead.

On Sunday, Kitty's television set went haywire. The duty nurse called Claire at noon.

"Your mother is having a tantrum because her TV set isn't working."

Claire sighed wearily. "Can't she watch the one in the recreation room?"

"Yes, but she doesn't want to. She wants to watch her own set. When I tried to take her to the rec room, she kicked me. You're going to have to get hers fixed, Ms. Kendrick."

A sharp pain pierced Claire's temple. Repairing TV sets cost money. Money she didn't have.

"Don't worry, Mrs. Kenny. I'll bring my set in. Just give me an hour, okay?"

An hour and a half later, Claire hefted her portable TV set from the trunk of her car and lugged it into the nursing home. She fully expected to hear Kitty complaining and carrying on, but when she reached her mother's room, Kitty was happily ensconced in a big armchair, raptly watching figure skating on a new-looking color set.

Bewildered, Claire said, "Mom?"

Kitty turned and grinned, her green eyes filled with excitement. "See my new TV?" She pointed to the set.

"Where did it come from?"

But Kitty had turned back to the program.

The duty nurse shrugged when Claire quizzed her. "I have no idea. All I know is about fifteen minutes ago, this set was delivered."

"Who delivered it?"

"I don't know."

"Didn't they say anything?"

Mrs. Kenny frowned. "No. I thought you ordered it."

Claire suddenly knew the set had come from Nick. How he'd known about her mother's set breaking down, she had no idea.

"Well, she can't keep it."

The nurse looked at Claire as if she thought Claire were crazy, but she didn't say anything.

Later, after substituting her own portable for the new set—over Kitty's protests—Claire struggled to carry it out to her car.

But the next morning, when she called Nick's office and Wanda put him on the line, he denied all knowledge of the set.

"Fine," she snapped. "I'll just bring it into work and deposit it on your desk, then."

But of course she knew she wouldn't. She certainly didn't want anyone at work to know what was happening.

Two days later, her car wouldn't start. Claire felt like sitting down in the parking lot and crying. *Please, God. Don't do this to me.* Shoulders slumping, she climbed the stairs back to her apartment and called the corner service station.

Fifteen minutes later the mechanic from the station pulled into the parking lot. He tinkered with the car for a few minutes, then wiped his hand across his forehead. "Ms. Kendrick, I'm sorry, but it looks to me like it's your alternator."

"How much?"

When he told her, she cringed. Getting her car fixed would wipe out every penny of her savings, which wasn't much to begin with. And she'd been saving that money to buy new tires, which she needed desperately. But what could she do?

Hours later, Claire stared out the window of her office. She felt so inadequate. Suddenly, everything seemed too much for her. She felt exactly like the little Dutch boy must have felt when he stuck his finger in the dike.

That night, Peachey picked her up. She had also driven her into work that morning. "You're a wonderful friend, you know that?" Claire said as she slid into the front seat of Peachey's sporty little Mazda.

"Come on, Claire. It's not a big deal."

"It is to me."

"When's your car going to be ready?"

"Tomorrow."

"I'll take you to pick it up."

The next day, when they arrived at the service station, Clyde, the mechanic, handed her the work order to look over. "I did everything you asked for. I'm sure glad you decided to have the works." He beamed at her.

"The works. What do you mean?" Alarm caused her voice to squeak.

"You know, new tires, replace those worn belts, fix the A.C., get that alignment taken care of—the works." Clyde's smile faded as he watched her face.

"Clyde, I never authorized you to do that."

He scratched his head, his light blue eyes puzzled. "Sure you did. I have the work order right here." He pointed to the paper in her hand. "Why, that fella from your office, he said—"

"What fella from my office?"

Clyde shrugged. "I dunno. Somebody called here yesterday, said he was from your office, told us to fix everything that needed fixin' on your car and to put four new tires on it."

Nick! Who else could it have been? Anger, hot and thick, clogged her throat. Damn him! Damn him.

"Clyde, I can't afford all of this. I . . . I'm sorry, but there's been a mix-up. I can't pay for all this work."

"The bill's already been taken care of, Ms. Kendrick."

Claire looked at Peachey.

Peachey raised her eyebrows.

Claire, teeth clenched, didn't say another word. All the way home, she alternated between swearing at Nick and marveling at how good her car sounded. She knew if she called him he'd deny everything.

Sure enough, he did. "I don't know what you're talking about, Claire," he said.

The worst part of these two incidents was that Claire could feel herself weakening. And she didn't want to weaken.

The following day he started working on her through Kitty. On Thursday night, when Claire showed up at Pinehaven, tired and worried because it was now February and March 1st was looming closer every day, Kitty was eating Godiva chocolates and there was a huge bouquet of flowers sitting on her nightstand.

"Where did these come from?" Claire asked Amy.

Amy shrugged. "I don't know. They were delivered earlier today."

Claire couldn't even get angry. Especially when she saw how much pleasure they had given Kitty. After all, what right did she have to deny her mother the little pleasure she did have? After that, each day Kitty received a present of some kind: a bracelet, a bottle of Joy, candy, a stuffed animal, a lace-edged handkerchief, a lovely handpainted scarf, a porcelain music box.

Kitty was ecstatic.

Claire was tired.

So tired, she thought, as she drove home from the nursing home. Tired of resisting what Nick was offering her. Tired of trying to find a way out of her problem.

Tired of being alone. Tired of trying and trying and never getting anywhere. Tired of everything.

She wasn't sure how much longer she could hold out. She wasn't sure if she even wanted to hold out. What was she trying to prove anyway? Why shouldn't she grab this opportunity he was offering? After all, he'd made things very clear. All he wanted was for her to keep his home life peaceful and give him children.

Children. A painful lump formed in Claire's chest. Tomorrow she would try to reason with him one last time. Because if he kept this up much longer, she didn't think she was strong enough to resist.

The next morning she called Nick's secretary to see if he would have time to see her.

"He'll see you at ten o'clock," Wanda said.

Promptly at ten, Claire presented herself on the 50th floor. When she walked into Nick's office, he smiled and stood. "Well, this is a nice surprise."

"Nick, I've come to ask you to stop. What you're doing isn't fair, especially to my mother. It's not right to let her get used to these luxuries. In fact, it's cruel."

"There's no reason these luxuries, as you call them, have to stop."

When she met his gaze, she expected to see arrogance, that same cocksure look she'd seen so many times before. Instead, she saw concern and kindness and something else, something that made her stomach feel hollow. "There's a perfectly good reason, and you know it."

He sighed. "Claire, give me a chance. That's all I'm asking. Go out with me Saturday night. Let me show you my proposition can work."

Because she was so tired and feeling so vulnerable,

she answered more harshly than she'd intended to. "No. I won't go out with you."

"I could make you, you know. After all, I am your boss."

Claire jumped up. "I can't believe you'd resort to blackmail!"

"Whatever it takes," he said, his voice light and teasing.

"Win at any price. Is that it?" She was so angry she could hardly talk.

"I told you once before. I rarely lose."

He looked so smug, so supremely sure of himself.

"Well, Mr. Callahan, if you think I'm going to do whatever you tell me to do simply because you own this company, you're dead wrong. Because I won't. No matter how many orders you give me. And if you don't like it, I guess you'll just have to fire me."

Before she reached the door, Nick was at her side, grasping her arm. She yanked it free and glared at him.

He spoke softly. "All right. You're fired. Now will you marry me?"

SIX

For a long moment, they stared at each other. Thoughts tumbled through Claire's mind with the turbulence of a jet-propelled engine. She wanted to smack the self-assurance right off his handsome, arrogant face. Her chest heaved and her face felt hot.

His molten-blue eyes were sparked with emotion: amusement and something else, something that flashed between them in a sizzling arc. Claire was reminded of the night in New Orleans when they stood outside her hotel room door and she'd known he wanted to kiss her.

He wanted to kiss her now.

The knowledge thrummed between them.

He wanted to kiss her.

And she wanted him to.

Oh, you're in big trouble, she told herself, stunned by the strength of the awareness between them.

"Why are you fighting me, Claire?"

Good question. Why *was* she fighting him? He was

offering her everything she'd ever wanted: security, freedom from worry, children. So what if he wouldn't promise undying love? She had never expected marriage, let alone love. He obviously desired her physically.

And that thought excites you. Admit it.

Okay, she would be honest with herself. She *was* excited by him. He fascinated her and made her feel like a woman.

So why shouldn't she enter into this sensible bargain? Holding out like this, for some kind of misguided principle, would cause Kitty to suffer needlessly and for what? For nothing.

She shrugged. A permanent tiredness had seeped into her bones. His question was legitimate. *Why was she fighting him?* "I don't know."

This time, when he touched her arm, she let him lead her back into the office. He guided her to the far corner where two couches were placed at right angles to one another, with a low coffee table centered in front of them.

Claire sat on one of them. He sat on the other. For a few moments, he was silent. The entire office was silent except for the muted sounds on the other side of the heavy walnut doors. The 50th floor was completely insulated, Claire thought. Insulated and protected. Exactly the way her life would be if she married him.

He leaned forward, arms resting on his knees as he studied her. "Claire, will you answer a few questions for me?"

"That depends on the questions."

"Fair enough." One corner of his mouth lifted. "First question: If I had never mentioned marriage to you—what would you think of me?"

"I . . . I'm not sure what you mean." What kind of game was he playing now?

"What would you think of me? Would you dislike me? Would you dislike being with me?"

"No." She shook her head. "No. I . . ." She broke off, met his eyes. So blue. They were so blue.

"Well?" he said softly.

"I . . . I wouldn't . . . I don't dislike you." She wasn't sure she liked him either. This emotion she felt whenever she was with him was too strong to be described by such an innocuous word as *like*.

"Do you respect me?"

"I did before all this started."

"Do you enjoy being with me?"

"Most of the time."

"So, if I had not mentioned marriage and asked you to go out with me—just an ordinary date—would you have gone?"

She wanted to say no.

Their eyes met again. The clock on his credenza struck the half hour, its soft chimes keeping time with Claire's heartbeat. She couldn't seem to look away.

"Would you have gone?" he asked again.

"Yes."

"I enjoy being with you, too," he said quietly. "I think we could have a good marriage."

She licked her lips. His eyes followed the movement. She took a deep breath. The moment seemed suspended in time. "All right. I'll marry you."

His eyes flashed with triumph, and Claire, unable to look away, shivered. Fear and excitement coursed through her. What had she done?

Grinning, he stood, then walked over to his desk. He unlocked a bottom drawer, removed something, then walked back toward her. Solemnly, he handed her a small velvet box.

Dazed, Claire lifted the lid and gasped. Nestled into the satin lining was an enormous round diamond solitaire. Her heart pounded. Had he been so sure she'd say yes? She wanted to be angry with him for this blatant display of confidence. But how could she be mad? The very qualities that angered her were the ones that had made him the successful man he was.

The man who's going to make your mother's life and your life safe. The man who's offering to share his life, his home, and his fortune. The man who's been honest about his feelings.

Wordlessly, she looked up. Nick took the box from her limp fingers, removed the ring, and slipped it on her left hand, holding her fingers lightly. Even this casual touch started a trembling in her stomach, and she could hardly meet his eyes.

The ring was loose, and he said, "Tomorrow we'll go to the jeweler's together and get this sized for you."

Claire looked at the ring glittering on her finger. It was magnificent. Raising her eyes to meet his warm gaze, she said, "It's very beautiful. But I never expected—"

"I know that. If you'd expected it, it wouldn't have given me nearly as much pleasure to give it to you."

Then, before she could say anything else, he slipped his arms around her, lowered his head, and kissed her.

Claire felt as if she were on a merry-go-round as she clung to him. The kiss drew all her strength from her body and caused her blood to heat and her heart to pound. She could feel his hands holding her tightly, their heat searing her through the thin silk of her dress.

He broke the kiss, finally, then said huskily, "You won't be sorry, Claire. I promise you that."

And with his ring glittering on her finger, and his promise echoing in her heart, Claire prayed he was right.

At seven o'clock the next morning, Claire called Peachey. "Help," she said. "Please come over. I have to talk to you."

"Come over! It's the middle of the night."

"Peachey, I need you."

Claire heard Peachey's moan. "Okay. Say no more." Then Peachey chuckled. "Can I take a shower first?"

"Yes."

"Put on the coffee. I'll be there in an hour."

True to her word, Peachey arrived at Claire's door fifty-eight minutes later. She looked gorgeous, Claire thought, for someone who'd been rousted out of bed hours before she normally woke up. She was wearing black tights and a long red T-shirt with sparkley stuff all over it, her silver fox coat slung carelessly over her shoulders. From her small ears hung red crystal waterfall earrings, the longest Claire had ever seen.

"Where's that coffee?" Peachey demanded.

Claire handed her a cup and pointed toward the coffee maker.

"Ahhh, ambrosia," Peachey declared as she took her first sip. "Now, what couldn't wait?"

"Oh, Peachey, I *had* to talk to you. I . . . I told Nick Callahan I'd marry him." She thrust her left hand under Peachey's nose. The diamond flashed with fiery brilliance.

Peachey's eyes widened and she whistled. "Holy Christmas! Are you tryin' to knock my eyes out? That rock must be three carats, at least!'' She took Claire's hand and turned it from side to side as she appraised the ring. ''I can't even imagine how much this thing cost. It looks like a perfect yellow diamond and those babies are rare.'' She sighed. ''I'd sell my soul to own one of these.'' Then her eyes narrowed and she put her hands on her hips. ''I thought you told me you weren't going to marry him.''

Claire couldn't meet Peachey's eyes. She fiddled with her coffee cup and said softly, ''I had a change of heart.''

''So I see . . .'' Peachey tapped her long, red fingernails against the laminated surface of Claire's round dining table. ''And what brought on this change of heart?''

Claire sighed. ''Oh, Peachey. I don't know. I thought I had everything all figured out. But yesterday, suddenly, I was just so tired. I kept thinking about my mother, about how happy we used to be. And the more I thought about her, the more I wondered if I was being selfish. After all, lots of people marry for reasons other than love. There's no disgrace in it.''

Peachey didn't say anything, just looked at her over the rim of her coffee cup. Her eyes reminded Claire of shiny black onyx as they silently studied her.

Claire squirmed. ''Say something.''

Peachey smiled and put down her cup. ''So you're telling me that you accepted Nick Callahan's offer strictly because of your mother.''

''Yes . . .''

''And not because you're the least little bit attracted to the man.''

Claire thought about the way she'd felt when Nick

kissed her. How she'd wanted him to kiss her. She could feel her face heating. "I—"

"Sugar, if you want to lie to yourself, go right ahead. But this is Peachey, your number-one best friend. I know you too well to believe that you'd marry this guy just to secure your mother's future." She grinned, her eyes sparkling in the morning sunlight. "If you're really going through with this marriage, it's because you're half in love with him already."

Claire sighed as she gave herself a final inspection that evening. She smoothed down the skirt of her dark green dress. All day she'd thought about what Peachey had said. Was Peachey right? *Was* she half in love with Nick? She shivered as she remembered the expression in his eyes yesterday as they'd stood by his office door.

She hoped she was doing the right thing. She wished she could talk to her mother. If only Kitty could tell her how she felt. But her mother had been a hopeless romantic. Would Kitty tell her not to marry Nick?

Why was it so hard for Claire to let go of that last slender thread of a dream of a marriage like her parents had shared? Her parents had been so happy together. Claire closed her eyes, images from earlier days crowding together in her mind. Her father, bringing home a bunch of daisies and Kitty running to meet him, her eyes sparkling with joy and love. The way he'd sneak up behind her mother when Kitty was in the kitchen, snake his arms around her waist, and lower his head to kiss and nibble on her neck. Kitty would blush and giggle and say, "John, stop it," but Claire knew her mother liked it. And Claire liked it, too. She liked the warm, happy feeling she got in her stomach when she watched her parents together. They made her feel safe and special and loved.

If she married Nick, what would their life together be like? Would she ever know times of intense happiness, the kind of happiness her parents had known, without having the kind of love they'd had? Could she share a physical relationship without sharing an emotional one? Could she make love with Nick if they weren't in love?

Tonight would be their first night together as an engaged couple. She squeezed her eyes shut. Right or wrong, she'd made up her mind. She wouldn't change it.

Her doorbell rang promptly at seven. Her heart began to race. Taking a deep breath, she put a bright smile on her face and opened the door. She was startled to see Nick's driver standing there.

"Gordon!"

"Mr. Callahan asked me to pick you up," Gordon said.

"Oh." This was different, Claire thought as she put on her lined raincoat and picked up her purse. She knew that Nick had a fascination with expensive and beautiful cars and normally preferred to drive himself around in the evenings. He'd told her he owned a silver Lotus, a black Jaguar, a red Maserati, and a dark blue Porsche.

"Where are we going, Gordon?" she asked.

"My instructions are to take you to Mr. Callahan's home, Ms. Kendrick."

Mr. Callahan's home. Her stomach fluttered as she thought about spending the evening in the intimacy of Nick's home. Thirty minutes later, as they pulled into the circular driveway, and Claire got her first look at the River Oaks mansion, she smiled a wry smile. Intimate? This great sand-colored brick edifice looked more like a medieval castle than an intimate home—complete with circular tower at one end. All it needed was a moat, she thought, as Gordon helped her from the car and up the shallow front steps to the double mahogany doors.

As they reached the top step, the doors opened wide, and a smiling maid greeted them. Within moments, Claire was ushered into an immense formal living room and Nick was walking forward to greet her. He took her hands, smiling down at her, and her breath caught. He was wearing a soft suede jacket in a beautiful shade of cinnamon with a creamy open-necked shirt underneath.

He bent to brush her cheek in greeting, and his cologne, something that smelled of mountains and forests, drifted over her. "Welcome to my home," he said.

Although her stomach felt hollow, she spoke lightly. "You took it literally, didn't you?"

He frowned, a quizzical smile on his face. "Took what literally?"

"A man's home is his castle."

He laughed out loud. "It *is* ridiculous, isn't it?"

"Actually, I'm impressed. As a little girl, I loved fairy tales, and this place really reminds me of the castle Rapunzel lived in. I can just see her up in that tower with her hair hanging down."

He continued to chuckle. "Well, good. I'm glad this place appeals to you. After all, it's going to be your home soon."

Her home. Their home. Claire evaded his eyes. She could feel herself blushing.

Nick motioned to one of the leather sofas on either

side of the fireplace. "Would you like a glass of wine?"

For Claire, the rest of the evening passed in a blur of sensory images: the crackle and hiss of the fire burning brightly in the great stone fireplace; the sensuous feel of the butter-soft leather covering the deep-cushioned sofas; the rich patina of the polished oak tables; the combined scents of furniture polish, fresh cut flowers, and burning cedar; the jewel tones of the beautiful Oriental carpets covering the stone-tiled floor; the sparkle of the crystal decanter as Nick poured her a glass of wine; the poetry of Mozart's "Eine Kleine Nachtmusik" playing softly in the background; the glow of candlelight over Nick's rugged, tanned face; and then later, the delicious dinner of lamb and new potatoes and tiny creamed peas; the tang of dark burgundy wine; the tinkle of silver against china; the whispery footsteps of the dark-haired maid who served them; and always, always, the vibrant blue of Nick's eyes as they watched her with an intoxicating intensity.

All Claire's doubts, all her problems receded, and she allowed herself to fall under the spell of the magical house.

And after dinner, when Nick took her on a tour, Claire felt more and more as if she'd entered a time warp. The rooms were all high-ceilinged and filled with priceless antiques and rich, beautiful fabrics and upholstery. Breathtaking Impressionist paintings glowed from the walls. Everywhere Claire looked she saw elegance and grace and beauty. And this was Nick's home. The home they would soon share.

And then he took her into the tower. The bottom level of the tower was a beautiful room that was obviously Nick's study.

"I've saved the best for last," he said, guiding her to the stairway in the middle of the room.

With him behind her, Claire climbed a twisting circular stairway to the room at the top. She took one look and fell hopelessly in love with the exquisite room circled by wide windows on all sides. It was furnished as a sitting room, and there was an intricately carved writing desk positioned under one of the windows, a Tiffany lamp throwing a circle of golden light on its shining top. Like a woman in a trance, Claire walked slowly over to the desk and rubbed her fingertips across the burnished surface.

A bittersweet yearning filled her. She could see herself sitting at the desk, writing letters and gazing out the window, daydreaming about . . . Nick. She could see herself curled up on one of the chintz-covered window seats, reading and listening to music while she waited for him to finish the work he'd brought home and climb the stairs to join her. She could see them sitting together on the plush loveseat while they discussed their respective days. She could see his dark head dipping as he nuzzled her neck . . . his strong, tanned hand moving up her ribcage to touch her. . . .

"It's wonderful," she said, hardly able to speak, her heart lodged somewhere in her throat, her breasts tingling from the imagined caress. She couldn't meet his eyes. She was afraid he'd know exactly what she'd been thinking.

"It's even better this way," he said softly. He reached to shut off the lamp. Suddenly, the room was a part of the navy night. Moonlight pooled at their feet, and everywhere Claire looked she could see stars. When he gently turned her to face him, his eyes glittering in the dark, she offered no resistance. How could she? This was what she'd been thinking about.

She closed her eyes and lifted her face, and when his cool, firm lips met hers, she sighed, her breath mingling with his.

He kissed her gently at first, his lips just grazing hers, his hands on either side of her face. But then the kiss grew more insistent, and he drew her closer, fitting her body tightly along the length of his. His mouth was heat and warmth and dark delight, and as the kiss deepened, desire spiraled through her as she arched against him. She shuddered as his hands stroked her, igniting nerve endings wherever they touched.

The kiss went on and on, and she felt as if she were one with the stars surrounding them—a shooting star rocketing through the universe. All thought disappeared. There was only the taste and smell and feel of Nick: holding her, kissing her, claiming her, and the starry night around them, closing them in its velvet embrace.

"Claire," he finally whispered, breaking the kiss, his breathing ragged. "Beautiful Claire." His lips dropped to her neck.

Claire's head spun. "Nick, I—"

He straightened. Very gently, he placed one finger against her lips. "Shhh. Not tonight. Tomorrow is soon enough to talk, don't you think?" And then he took her hand and led her down the steps and out of the tower to the entry hall. "Wait here." He disappeared and Claire tried to get her chaotic emotions under some semblance of control.

Her senses were still reeling from his devastating kiss, but she knew she had to pull herself together. She couldn't let him see how much his kiss had affected her. Minutes later, he returned, carrying her coat. As he held it up, then helped her put it on, his hands lingered on her shoulders just a moment longer than necessary, and Claire's traitorous heart skittered around in her chest.

But he didn't try to kiss her again. And all the way home, as she sat only inches away from him in the dark intimacy of the Lotus, he didn't once try to touch her. Instead, he inserted a cassette into the tape player and as the delicate strains of Debussy's "Claire de Lune" surrounded them, he said softly, "Put your head back and relax. It's been a long day."

When they reached her apartment, he helped her out of the car and followed her up the steep steps to her apartment. Claire's breathing quickened as she turned to say good-bye. As their eyes met, all she could think about was how it had felt to be held in his arms, to have him kiss her.

"Good-night, Claire," he murmured. "Sweet dreams."

"Good-night, Nick." Her heart thundered in her chest as his head dipped. She closed her eyes. But his lips just brushed her cheek.

"I'll call you tomorrow," he said. And then he was gone.

SEVEN

"You're what?"

Nick gave Tim a level look. "You heard me."

"But I can't believe I heard you correctly!"

"What can't you believe about it?" Nick twirled his pen between his fingers. He thought about the weekend and smiled.

"You can't be serious. You're joking, right?"

"I'm not joking. On Friday night Claire Kendrick accepted my proposal of marriage. Yesterday, we finalized the details. We're planning to be married in June."

"Nick!" Tim shoved his hair back from his forehead, his action a giveaway to his agitation. "Are you nuts? You've known the woman less than a month." He grimaced. "I thought that angel-faced innocence of hers was too good to be true, and it looks as if I'm right. She certainly is a fast worker. I can't believe she managed to fool you, and so quickly."

"She didn't fool me. This is completely my doing," Nick said mildly. He wasn't angry. He'd expected this

111

reaction from Tim, who had some idea he was Nick's protector. "I've thought it over very carefully. She suits me perfectly." He went on to explain the terms he and Claire had agreed upon the previous afternoon. He smiled remembering Claire's reaction to his plans. It pleased him that she seemed to expect so little. In his experience most people were out for all they could get, but Claire seemed to be that rarity—a person without greed.

"Wait a minute. Let me get this straight. You're telling me this is strictly a business relationship? Christ, Nick, you could have any woman you wanted. You don't have to bargain for a wife."

"All the women I know want to control me . . . and my money."

"And you think this Kendrick woman is any different?"

"I know she is."

Once more, Tim thrust his fingers through his hair. "Damn it, you're stubborn."

"So you've told me before."

"Nick, why are you doing this?"

"I've already told you. I want a wife. I want a home life. I want children."

"But why this way? Why marry someone you barely know and don't pretend to love?"

Nick smiled sardonically. Tim was a romantic. Under the bluster and legal brilliance and prudence, Tim was the kind of man who really believed in fairy tales and happy endings. "Of all people, you know better than anyone what a disaster my marriage to Jill was."

"Don't pile one mistake on top of another, then."

"This isn't a mistake." Nick rose, walked to the buffet server and poured himself a cup of the fresh coffee Wanda kept in plentiful supply. He considered his words carefully. Because Tim's friendship meant a lot to him, he wanted him to understand. "Every goal I've ever set for myself, I've met, with one exception."

Tim leaned back in his chair.

"My personal life has never been successful." Just saying the words out loud made Nick feel unsure of himself, a feeling he despised. Uncertainty was for the meek, the weak, those afraid to take what they wanted from life. He'd vowed long ago, when he'd been shunted from one foster home to another, that he'd be strong, as strong as necessary, and he'd never be afraid to go after what he wanted.

When Tim still said nothing, Nick continued, "I'm forty-two years old. If I'm ever to have a family, I'd better get started." He grinned. "I don't want to be the oldest man in the P.T.A." Then he became serious again. "For the past several years, I've been looking for a suitable wife. The search has been futile. Finally, I realized the reason I was having no success was because I wasn't approaching the problem the way I tackle difficulties in business. As soon as I realized I had to apply the same successful strategy to my personal goals, everything became clear to me."

"So you decided to buy a wife?"

"Why not acquire a wife the same way I'd acquire a company? Look over her assets, her liabilities, her strengths and weaknesses, see how we might complement one another, what she can offer me as well as what I can offer her?"

Tim shook his head. "I'm not believing this."

"It makes perfect sense when you think about it. The reason my personal life has been such a failure is I've allowed emotions to rule rather than sound reasoning. That's why I lost my edge. That's why I failed.''

"Well, I think you're destined to fail this time, too.''

"Why?''

"Because in your zeal, you forgot one of the cardinal rules of business. Cover your ass.''

Nick frowned.

"Think about it,'' Tim said. "You want me to draw up a contract that protects both her and her mother no matter what happens in the future. What about you?''

"What about me?''

"What about your protection?''

"I don't need protection from Claire,'' Nick said, beginning to get irritated.

"I say you do. As your legal counsel, I say if you're insistent about going through with this scheme, at the very least you need a full-fledged prenuptial agreement that not only spells out what you're going to do for her but guarantees what will happen if she doesn't live up to her end of the bargain.''

It irritated Nick that Tim was right. Nick couldn't imagine entering into any other kind of business deal without a written contract. Perhaps in the old days a man could depend upon another's word, but this was the twentieth century and things were no longer so simple.

"If this really *is* a business deal, then surely you see the advisability of doing it perfectly. As a matter-of-fact, I don't think you should sign anything until Ms. Kendrick has a physical examination. How do you even know she can have children?''

Damn. He should have thought of that himself. What if she *couldn't* have children? Reluctantly, he said, "I know you're right. Okay. Set it up.''

"Will she agree to it?"

"Yes. I'm sure she will."

Tim jotted some notes on the legal pad he held. "We'd better make this agreement airtight. If we don't, and something should go wrong, this dame could take you to the cleaners."

Nick stiffened. "Don't call her a dame. Her name is Claire," he said tightly.

Tim's brown eyes met his for a long moment. "All right. Sorry. Anyway, Claire could marry you, have your kid, divorce you, then take the kid as well as half of what you own."

Nick hated to admit Tim was right on all counts. Although he didn't want to believe Clarie would ever renege on a promise, people *did* change. Sometimes even the best intentions evaporated when things didn't go the way you expected them to go. He sighed. "You're right. Get started on drawing up the contract."

Tim rose. "Good. But I still think this is the craziest idea you've ever had."

Claire liked Nick's doctor. At first, she'd balked at having the physical, but after thinking about it, she realized Nick's request was reasonable. If, for some reason, she was unable to bear children, he had to know. So she kept the appointment, had the physical, and was told she was in perfect health.

"I see no reason why you can't have a dozen children," Dr. Ardale said. "You're a very healthy young woman."

Claire left the office knowing Nick would be pleased when he received the report from the doctor.

She was still walking around in a kind of rosy glow, even though she'd had ten days to get used to her new status as Nick Callahan's fiancée. At least once every thirty minutes she'd lift her hand, moving it back and forth so her engagement ring would catch the light, watching the way it sparkled with fiery brilliance. From the day she'd said she would marry him, her life had turned upside down, each day bringing some new delight to savor.

Nick had insisted that everything concerning their engagement and wedding be done exactly right. She thought back over the long conversation they'd had the Sunday after she accepted his offer. They had spent hours discussing how and when each event would take place. Claire envisioned a small wedding, but Nick had other ideas.

"We'll have an official engagement party in two weeks. Can you give my secretary a list of the people you'd like invited by Tuesday?"

An official engagement party? What would she wear? But in a few minutes, that question was answered.

"Tomorrow I'll have Wanda call the different shops and establish a line of credit for you." He mentioned places Claire had only read about—shops that carried designer labels where one item might cost more than her entire wardrobe. "You're going to need a lot of clothes because many of my friends and business associates will want to have parties for us. You'll also need a couple of furs, but don't buy jewelry. That's something I'll take care of."

As if she would have, Claire thought, totally bemused.

"I'll also have Wanda investigate and recommend a bridal consultant for you to work with. With someone good you should be able to have everything done and ready for a June wedding. What do you think?"

Claire didn't know what she thought. Her mind was whirling.

"My sister Natalie will be coming in for the engagement party. She lives in Los Angeles."

Claire remembered reading somewhere that he had a sister. But her research into his background had yielded little else about his private life.

"When you go into work tomorrow, give Ken Boudreaux your two weeks' notice. You're going to be too busy to work from now until the wedding."

"I don't want to quit working!" Claire protested.

"You won't have enough time to get ready for the wedding if you continue to work. Besides," he added, "it wouldn't be fair to my other employees to have you there. It would put them in an awkward position." He smiled, which took the sting from his words. "Didn't you realize you'd have to give up your job if you married me?"

"I . . . I guess I hadn't thought that far ahead," Claire admitted. He was right, she knew he was right. But she didn't have to like it. She began to feel as if a steamroller were mowing her down. Her carefully disciplined life was toppling faster than she could keep up with it.

So she'd given her notice, and now she only had three more days to work. And in four days, the big engagement party would take place. My second big hurdle, she thought, knowing she'd leaped the first with her positive report from the doctor.

She looked at her engagement ring again. Prisms of light and color dazzled her.

There would be a lot of hurdles to get over in the next months, she knew, but only one really frightened her: her wedding night.

Could she pull it off? Could she make love with Nick without love between them, without letting her own emotions go out of control? Because Claire had decided that no matter what her feelings were, she would stick to the spirit of their agreement. She knew if she allowed her emotions to rule her, she would put a strain on their relationship. He would begin to feel guilty because he couldn't offer her love, and then her position would be untenable. He might even begin to avoid her.

No, Claire thought. I want this marriage to work. I want him to feel comfortable around me. I don't want him to regret his decision to marry me. I've made a bargain and I'll stick to it. And if that means keeping my feelings hidden, so be it.

The party was going quite well, Nick thought, as he watched Claire talking to his sister, Natalie. With half an ear turned to Howard St. Martin's excruciatingly boring description of his latest African safari, he murmured encouragement at appropriate intervals, but his attention was centered on Claire.

She looked heart-stoppingly beautiful tonight. Her sea-green chiffon and lace dress was the perfect foil for her Dresden china beauty. He'd hardly been able to tear his eyes away from her since the moment she'd stepped across the threshold and into his home. When she'd smiled, shrugging out of her sheared beaver jacket, one of three furs he'd insisted she buy, and he saw her in the gossamer dress studded with tiny pearls, she had taken his breath away. The smile was radiant and he'd felt a surge of pride and possessiveness, knowing he was responsible for her obvious happiness. Her face glowed; she looked healthy and rested. Gone were the dark circles that she'd worn throughout the weeks she'd worried about her mother and her financial problems.

Now, as he watched her with Natalie, he was struck by the difference between the two women, yet pleased that they had seemed to like one another instantly. Natalie, like him, was tall, thin, and dark. Her gleaming ebony hair held a hint of silver at the temples and she was deeply tanned. Unlike his eyes, which he'd inherited from their mother, she had the dark brown eyes of their father. Natalie fairly vibrated energy and enthusiasm. She was a non-stop talker and a chain-smoker, a habit Nick had tried to get her to give up. He knew her husband, a brilliant neurosurgeon, had tried equally hard, but Natalie resisted all their blandishments.

"It's my body," she said stubbornly, dark eyes flashing.

Tonight, she looked striking in a black and white taffeta dress with dramatic lines that emphasized her angular, model's figure. To look at her, no one would ever guess what her background was. She looked like a jaded, petted, rich woman who had never done anything harder than play a rousing game of tennis. Nick smiled, remembering how different their lives used to be, how much he owed his sister. How much he would always owe her.

Now that he thought about it, she and Claire were alike in the important ways. Each had a fierce love of family and a strong sense of loyalty. And neither was afraid of hard work.

Now Claire laughed at something Natalie was saying, and Nick watched the way she tipped her head up and slightly to the side. Nick's breathing quickened as his eyes swept down the long line of her throat and rested on the sweep of her rounded breasts. She looked so cool, so elegant, so classically pure.

He smiled to himself. He had wondered if Claire, with her outward look of serenity, would be a responsive lover. He would have been able to live with it if she were passive, as long as she were willing. After all, the main reason he wanted a wife was to give him children. He didn't need passion as well.

But from the first moment he'd kissed her, he'd known she would be not only satisfying, but exciting and enthusiastic. In fact, the kiss had shaken him. He hadn't expected to enjoy it as much as he had, and he hadn't wanted to stop with the kiss. She'd been so sweetly willing and desire had raged through him, but he'd called on all his willpower and self-control to keep that desire banked. He had no intention of bedding her unless and until she was his legal wife. Tim might think he was crazy, but Nick was nobody's fool.

But soon she *would* be his wife. In three and one-half short months he would have the right to kiss her and touch her in all the hidden places, to take her mouth and her body and claim them for his own. To make slow love to her and watch her eyes as she flowered under his touch. To turn the cool, ladylike Claire into a trembling, eager lover.

"Nick, you're not listening," Howard said peevishly.

"What?" Nick looked at Howard, but his body felt taut with desire. The erotic images he'd conjured swirled in his mind and, suddenly, the months until his wedding day seemed like eternity.

"Well, Claire, when Nicky called me to tell me he was getting married, you could have knocked me over with a feather!"

Claire smiled at Natalie Burnstein. She couldn't get over how much she liked Nick's older sister. She'd been so nervous about meeting her, picturing someone who would be coldly suspicious of the unknown woman who had managed what so many women had been unable to pull off—snagging Nick Callahan. Claire knew that Nick hadn't told Natalie of their bargain. In fact, that had been one of Claire's conditions when they'd discussed the terms of their bargain. And he readily agreed, saying the only person who would know was Tim Sutherland, his lawyer, who was drawing up the prenuptial contract.

Natalie, although she fulfilled some of Claire's expectations—she was beautiful, sophisticated, intelligent, and charming—was also earthy, funny, and warmly accepting of Claire. From her first greeting, "Now I know exactly why Nicky finally succumbed," to her latest admission, she had been friendly, candid, and unabashedly nosy.

"But I'm tickled to death that he's getting married again," Natalie continued. "He *should* be married. He's the marrying kind."

Claire wondered what Natalie would think if she knew the true story.

"From the moment he and Jill were divorced, women have been chasing him. He's never been seriously interested in any of them." She grinned. "I call them the 'exes.' " Natalie opened her silk cigarette case and shook out a cigarette. She quickly lit it, took a long drag, and added, "His first marriage was a disaster, you know."

"Yes, well, he told me a little bit about it," Claire said.

"Jill's a nice woman, actually, but she was terribly possessive. Men need a little space."

Claire smiled, thinking, if you only knew.

"I have a feeling you're going to be good for him, though," Natalie continued. "Maybe now I can quit worrying about him." Then she glanced up. "Oh, no," she said out of the side of her mouth, "here comes one of the 'exes' now—Heather Richardson."

Claire recognized the beautiful redhead she'd met at the country club the night of the reception for the British consul-general. Heather looked very beautiful again tonight, in a sculpted gold tissue dress that showed off her lush curves.

"Hello, Natalie," Heather said. "It's good to see you again."

"Heather."

The two women touched cheeks. Then Heather's tawny eyes settled on Claire, and she smiled. "I guess congratulations are in order."

Before Claire could answer, Natalie said with mock reproof, "You're *never* supposed to congratulate the bride, Heather. It's the man who's considered the lucky one." She took a final drag on her cigarette, then stubbed it out in a large crystal ashtray.

"That may be," Heather said dryly, "but we all know that any woman who could land Nick Callahan deserves to be congratulated. It's quite a feat."

"Thank you," Claire said. "I *do* consider myself lucky."

"You definitely should. What we're all wondering is how you managed it . . . and so quickly, too."

Claire felt sorry for Heather—she knew the woman was in love with Nick—but she realized she would have to let Heather know she wasn't going to stand for insults or innuendos or anything else. So she gave Heather her sweetest smile and said, "You know how

Nick is. When he sees something he wants, he goes after it."

Heather's eyes narrowed. "Yes, I certainly *do* know how Nick is. I know that he'll stop at nothing to get what he wants. But I also know that he gets bored very quickly, too, once he's achieved his objective. So don't get too complacent."

Then she walked off, head high.

"Poor Heather," Natalie murmured. "She's eaten up with jealousy."

"Yes." But Claire was disturbed. How many people here tonight felt as Heather did? She hated the idea that there were people just hoping she'd fail, just waiting for something to happen and Nick to dump her. Some of this must have shown on her face, for Natalie spoke quietly.

"Claire, don't let what she said bother you. She really thought Nick was going to ask her to marry him, and she's very disappointed and envious."

But Claire's happiness in the evening had waned. She already knew Tim Sutherland disapproved of her. The suspicion she'd sensed the first day she'd met him in Nick's office had been evident again tonight. And now Heather.

"Come on, Claire," Natalie urged. "Smile. Don't give her the satisfaction of knowing she got to you. That's what she wants, to put doubts in your mind." Natalie poked her arm. "Besides, here comes Nicky."

And then Nick was at her side, smiling down at her, and the approval she saw in his eyes made her forget Heather Richardson and her snide comments, and relief washed over her. *I don't have to worry anymore. And I'll make him happy,* she vowed. *I'll never give him any reason to regret marrying me.* She gave him an answering smile.

"Good girl," Natalie whispered. Then she looked at Nick. "I'm really looking forward to the wedding. And I'll make sure David comes if I have to drag him here."

Impulsively, Claire said, "Natalie, would you like to be my matron of honor?"

Natalie's smile was dazzling. "I'd love it. Are you sure?"

Even though Claire had just thought of the idea, she was very sure. She nodded.

Natalie hugged her, and Claire glanced up at Nick. His blue eyes were shining, and she felt a warm glow at the thought that she'd pleased him.

"Who else is going to be in the wedding?" Natalie asked.

"My best friend, Peachey Hall, is going to be my maid of honor. I'm not planning to have any other attendants."

"Is your friend here tonight? I'd love to meet her."

"No," Claire said regretfully. "She's a model and she had a shoot scheduled in St. Thomas this week. She wanted to be here, but she couldn't—the agency booked her months ago."

"Well, I'm excited about this," Natalie said. "And I can't wait." She laughed. "And from the look on your fiancé's face, he can't wait, either."

"I'm counting the days," Nick said. He slipped his arm around her, resting it just under her breast. Claire was acutely aware of the heat of his hand through the thin dress, and suddenly her mouth went dry. He'd sounded as if he meant it. She slowly looked up, meeting his electric-blue gaze.

What she saw there totally unnerved her.

He might not be in love with her.

But his eyes said he wanted her.

_____ EIGHT _____

Claire stood in the back of the church waiting for the first notes of Purcell's "Trumpet Voluntary." Sunlight filtered through the stained-glass windows, bathing the assembled guests in jeweled rays of emerald, ruby, and sapphire. Claire took measured breaths, willing herself to relax, and stood motionless as the wedding coordinator adjusted her heavy train.

She couldn't see Nick from where she stood, but she knew he was up there by the altar, waiting for her. She closed her eyes for a moment. The heady fragrance of roses drifted around her.

Nick. Just thinking about him and the way he looked at her frightened her. She wasn't sure why. All his actions had been kind and considerate—just as he'd promised her they would be—but there was some secret part of himself he kept closed off from her. She wished she understood him better.

He wanted her physically. She knew that. She could see it in his eyes and in the way his body reacted whenever he kissed her. But even then, he was always in control. Claire knew their lives would follow this same pattern.

Nick would always be in charge. Always be in control. He would set the pace and she would follow. Each phase of their lives would be assessed, and he would then make an informed decision. Nothing would be spontaneous.

She sighed. This was her wedding day. Soon the ceremony uniting her to Nick would begin. It was too late for doubts. Finally Peachey, looking glamorous and sultry in her ice-blue watered silk dress, reached the altar and stopped, turning toward the center aisle.

For a moment there was a hush, then the minister raised his hands and the guests stood, amid rustling and expectant in-drawn breaths. The sunlight danced over their heads and then the full, rich tones of the organ filled the church.

Claire, head held high, right arm resting upon the sleeve of her Uncle Dale's arm, began her slow descent down the aisle toward her future.

Nick sucked in his breath when he saw her. She looked indescribably beautiful. Her dress was lush ivory satin with a sweeping train, elegant and simple with clean lines that emphasized her slender figure. She'd piled her golden hair on top of her head, and the head-piece of her veil was studded with sequins and pearls that shimmered in the filtered sunlight dappling the church.

A tremor passed through him as she came closer and he saw the luminous glow in her eyes, the sweetly vulnerable curve of her mouth, the delicate rose shading her cheekbones, and the soft rise and fall of her rounded breasts gilded by satin.

Mine, he thought. Mine. Pure and beautiful and malleable. At that moment, her soft green eyes met his and Nick smiled, seeing the way her eyes glowed in return. Claire, he thought. Beautiful Claire. He moved toward her and then the minister began to speak.

"This is quite a party, Claire," Betty O'Neil said.

Claire smiled at her former boss. "Yes. Nick said he felt obligated to have this type of reception. I'd have preferred something much smaller."

Betty smiled. "It's still hard for me to believe that you and Nick Callahan . . ."

Claire forced herself to smile. She was so tired of the speculative looks, the same old comments repeated over and over again. She knew Betty meant her no ill will, but each time someone expressed surprise or amazement over her marriage to Nick, Claire felt just a bit more uncertain, just a bit more apprehensive of the future. And she didn't like the feeling.

She wished the reception was over. The country club was lovely, the food magnificent, the champagne and wine costly and plentiful, the music and service topnotch, and she knew the guests were having a marvelous time—if the noise level and speed in which the food and drinks were disappearing were any indication—but Claire was too tense to enjoy herself.

Even Nick, who was solicitous and attentive to a fault, couldn't distract Claire's thoughts from her fear of the future, and the more immediate fear of tonight.

She swallowed. Tonight she and Nick would be alone, together, as man and wife. Tonight he would claim her. Suddenly she was terribly afraid. What if she didn't measure up? What if he didn't enjoy making love to her? What if he were sorry he'd married her?

What if, as Heather Richardson had so convincingly pointed out, he became bored with her?

Just as her thoughts took this dismal turn, her aunt Susan approached. Claire's spirits immediately lifted. Her mother's sister was one of her favorite people in the entire world. Today she looked lovely, Claire thought, in her pink silk suit and matching hat. Her silver hair, which had once been midnight dark, set off her green eyes, a family trademark.

"Claire, honey, you look so beautiful today," she murmured as they hugged for at least the tenth time that afternoon. "I was so proud when I saw you walking down the aisle. And I know your father and mother would have been, too."

Claire's eyes misted. She had so wanted Kitty to be there, but her doctors had adamantly refused, saying Kitty would be confused and get over-excited and make herself sick. Claire knew they were right, but still, something in her rebelled at the idea that her own mother didn't know she had gotten married today.

"Be happy, Claire," her aunt continued, holding her hands tightly and smiling at her with tear-filled eyes. "Be very, very happy. You deserve to be."

And I want to be. But I'm so afraid. Of course, she didn't say the words aloud. But they were there, lurking in the shadows of her mind, waiting to pounce.

Just then, Nick walked up to them. He smiled slowly, and Claire's heart turned over. He looked magnificent in his black tuxedo, as if he'd been born to wear it. He turned his smile on her aunt, saying, "Susan, do you mind if I steal my wife away for a dance?"

My wife. Claire's heart lifted with pride as the words washed over her. *My wife.* She allowed herself to be led to the dance floor, and as Nick drew her close and they began to move to the music, she glanced over at her aunt and smiled.

Susan smiled back. Then she nodded, almost imperceptibly, as if she were assuring Claire that everything would be okay.

Nick's arms tightened around her, and Claire nestled her head under his chin and closed her eyes. For better or for worse, she thought, I'm Nick's wife.

Later, Nick said, "Would you like to leave the reception early and go to see your mother?"

"Do you mean it?" Claire said.

His eyes softened. "Of course."

Heart full, she smiled up at him. She thought it was a hopeful sign for their future that he had been perceptive enough to know how she was feeling. So they said their good-byes, and when Claire turned to say good-bye to Susan, her aunt whispered, "He'll be good to you. He has kind eyes."

Ten minutes later, after being pelted by rice and good wishes, they were on their way, Claire's hand clasped warmly in Nick's, and Claire thought about her aunt's words as they sat in the back of the limo and Gordon drove them to Pinehaven.

They caused a stir when they entered the nursing home. The elderly patients oohed and aahed over Claire's wedding finery, and Claire was very grateful to Nick for his patience when the women clucked over him.

They found her playing with a doll's house in the rec room. Kitty's eyed widened when she saw them.

Her mouth curved in a delighted smile. "Pretty," she said, touching Claire's veil.

Claire's eyes filled with tears, and Nick put his arm around her shoulders. "Hi, Mom," she said. "This is Nick."

"Nick," Kitty said, her green eyes shining. She lowered her eyelashes in a coy gesture. "Nick."

"Hello, Kitty." Nick took her hand, raised it to his lips, and kissed it. "Now I see why Claire is so beautiful. She looks like her mother."

How kind he could be, Claire thought.

Kitty loved his attention, but her eyes kept returning to Claire's veil. Finally, she said, "Kitty wants the pretty hat."

Claire looked at Nick. He smiled, and the brilliance of his eyes dazzled her. "If it makes her happy, let her have it," he murmured.

So, with his help, Claire removed the delicate veil, and he helped her pin it to Kitty's hair. Their eyes met over Kitty's head, and in that moment, Claire knew Peachey hadn't been quite right. Claire wasn't half in love with her husband. She was all the way in love with him.

From Pinehaven, it was only a twenty-five minute ride to Nick's house, where their luggage was ready and waiting for them.

By seven, Claire was ready, dressed in comfortable violet silk loose-fitting pants and matching jacket over a white shell top. Nick, too, wore casually elegant clothes: gray slacks, open-necked pale blue shirt, and lightweight gray wool sports coat. Their matched luggage was already loaded into the limousine, and Nick was waiting for her.

As they rode to the airport, with her left hand Claire fingered the pearls at her throat—Nick's wedding gift to her—and with her right hand she absorbed the heat from his hand, which was once again holding hers firmly. His thumb absently rubbed the back of her hand, sending a frisson of awareness up her arm. Her mind throbbed with the realization of her true feelings for him.

"We'll be there soon," he murmured close to her hair, his warm breath sending a shiver down her spine. "Are you tired?"

Claire *was* tired, but she was also tense as a bow string. "A little."

"You can nap on the plane. Then, when we arrive in San Francisco, you'll be rested." He kissed her temple. "If I didn't tell you before, you looked beautiful today."

At his words, and the husky warmth in his voice when he said them, Claire felt as if someone had poured warm honey over her. She turned her head toward him, and they were so close, all she saw was the vivid blue of his eyes. When his moist mouth moved to cover hers, something hot and liquid curled into her stomach.

"I can't wait until tonight," he whispered against her slightly open mouth. The hand that wasn't holding hers slid under her silk jacket, stroking her rib cage, then moving up to cover her breast. His thumb rubbed against the tightened nub, and a piercingly sweet pain knifed through her. She arched against his hand and he kissed her again. Her head spun and she felt weak with wanting him.

He finally withdrew his hand, stroking her cheek instead, and Claire's breast ached from his touch. She closed her eyes and he kissed her eyelids, then dropped back down to her mouth, soothing her as his lips grazed hers. They finally drew apart, and his eyes were filled with promise as they studied her upturned face.

When he looked at her like that, she knew she'd give him anything he asked for. Anything. Anytime. Anywhere.

The company plane landed at San Francisco International Airport at nine o'clock that evening, San Francisco time. Claire, who had thought she'd be too nervous to sleep on the flight, had fallen asleep almost immediately after they were airborne. Nick woke her about thirty minutes before landing, and she'd had time to wash her face, freshen her makeup, and drink a cup of tea. She'd also been able to see the beauty of San Francisco at night as the plane circled over the city. Through the evening fog, a ribbon of tiny lights delineated the sweeping magnificence of the Golden Gate Bridge, and Claire felt her heart skitter with anticipation.

Callahan, International had an office in the Bay Area, Nick explained, as they were met by a limousine. Within moments, their baggage had been transferred to the sleek automobile and they were heading toward the city, cushioned in plush seats.

"For the first three or four nights, we'll stay at the St. Maurice," Nick said. "Then we'll go to the Monterey Peninsula, where I've rented a house. If you want to, we can even stay up in Napa for a couple of days." His hand rested lightly, but possessively, on her thigh.

Claire gave him a smile. Her head was whirling. For someone who'd hardly been anywhere, the prospect of staying in places she'd only read about or seen in the movies was exhilarating. And Nick's touch, with its promise of things to come, had her pulses racing.

The St. Maurice was everything she'd ever expected it to be. Old. Ornate. Elegant. And from the moment they stepped out of their limousine on Nob Hill onto the sidewalk in front of their hotel, they were given the red-carpet treatment. Claire had spent enough time with Nick to know this preferential treatment was the rule rather than the exception whenever he went anywhere, but she wasn't jaded enough not to appreciate it and bask in it.

Their suite was magnificent, she thought—on the top floor of the hotel, giving them a panoramic view of the city with the bay in the distance—with a private terrace complete with table and chairs for dining, chaise longues for napping or sunning, and flower filled boxes and tubs.

Sitting on the sideboard was a basket of fruit and a platter of paté and assorted cheeses and crackers. A bottle of wine was chilling in an ice bucket. Flowers were everywhere: roses, gardenias, camellias, and tiny baby orchids. The terrace doors stood open, and a fresh, cool breeze blew in, causing the sheer curtains to billow.

Claire saw the enormous sitting room with a marble fireplace, in front of which a small table was set for dining, and several doors leading to what she supposed were bedrooms, bathrooms, and dressing areas. Nick instructed the bellboy where to put their luggage, and Claire wandered to the open terrace doors. She walked outside and leaned against the railing. San Francisco, like a beautiful jewel, was spread before her. Lights twinkled below, and the muffled sounds of cars and a bustling city floated up on the night air. She shivered in her thin silk outfit; it was really too chilly to stand outside.

Just as she turned to go in, strong arms slipped around her, and Claire's heart lurched. She leaned back, into the embrace, and his arms tightened, spreading warmth and a delicious tingle through her as they crossed in front of her and rubbed her arms. His mouth was right next to her ear and when he spoke, his breath feathered her hair and caused her stomach to tighten.

"You're cold," he said softly. "Come inside."

His mouth slipped to her neck, and Claire shivered again, but this time the shiver wasn't caused by cold but by the heat filling her body as his lips nuzzled her neck then moved up to take her earlobe between his teeth and gently nip it.

"Come," he said again, taking her hand and leading her indoors. As if she had no will of her own, Claire followed him through the sitting room and into an enormous bedroom dominated by a king-size four poster bed draped in creamy lace and covered with an ornate lace spread that had been turned down invitingly. Claire's face felt hot as she stared at the bed. Hurriedly, she looked away.

Here in the bedroom the green satin drapes were drawn against the night and soft lamps glowed on the bedside tables. There was also a fireplace—a smaller version of the one in the sitting room area.

"I thought tonight, since it's late and it's been a long day, we'd have dinner here in our suite," he said.

Their eyes met, and Claire swallowed. "That sounds nice." She looked around. "I think I'll bathe and change then."

"Take your time," he said. "I'll use the other bathroom."

After he left her alone, she filled the huge tub with steaming, hot water and liberally laced it with scented bath salts. Then she slowly lowered herself into the water, luxuriating in the feel of it as it lapped over her. She fondly remembered the last time she'd soaked in a bath. For years, quick showers had been the norm—a necessity borne of too much to do in too little time. She laid her head back and closed her eyes. She felt pampered. She felt wonderful.

Later, refreshed and relaxed, she toweled herself dry with one of the thick green bath towels, warm from the warming rack, then used scented body lotion, rubbing it into her skin. Finally, scented and creamed, she drew on wispy yellow lace and satin panties, then a matching nightgown and peignoir. Finally, she slipped her feet into yellow satin slippers. Then she carefully brushed her hair and applied light makeup—just a touch of blush and lip gloss and a tiny bit of eye shadow and mascara.

She looked at herself in the bathroom mirror. What she saw was a beautiful woman with uncertain eyes and a nervous smile—a woman who was getting ready to go out and meet her husband—a woman who prayed she wouldn't disappoint him.

Nick couldn't take his eyes off her. Although he'd taken great pains to order the most delicious, tempting dinner he could think of, the only thing he wanted to taste was Claire. If anything, she looked even more beautiful than she'd looked in her wedding dress. The satin and lace gown and peignoir she wore clung to her body, outlining every curve, every hollow, every delectable inch. When she walked toward him, his heart lunged somewhere up in the vicinity of his throat as he saw the way the satin whispered over her skin and how the pale yellow color shimmered in the soft lights.

While she'd been bathing and changing, Nick, too,

had prepared himself for the coming night. First, he turned on the gas fire in the sitting room fireplace, then he did the same in the bedroom, smiling to himself as he heard Claire singing in the bathroom. Tiptoeing out, he went into the other bathroom and took a hot shower, toweled himself dry, splashed on a little cologne, then wrapped himself in a thick navy blue velour robe.

When their dinner arrived, he tipped the waiter generously and told him he'd take care of serving everything himself. He lit the candles on the small table near the fireplace, then uncorked the champagne, put in a compact disc of a Rachmaninoff concerto, and turned off most of the lights. Then he settled himself in front of the fire to wait.

And now his waiting was over.

Neither one of them ate very much. The lobster bisque, Ceasar salad, flaky croissants, grilled sole in lemon butter, new potatoes, and fresh asparagus might have been sawdust for all the attention they gave to the food.

They did drink the Moet Chandon, and Nick deliberately sipped at his slowly. Even though his body was tight with suppressed desire, even though he could hardly wait to take her in his arms, even though he wanted to make love to her more than he'd wanted anything in a long time—he also wanted to savor each moment, drawing out the anticipation so that his enjoyment, when it finally came, would be even greater.

He liked just looking at Claire. The firelight played over her face and hair, and Nick thought she looked like a young goddess sitting there in her beautiful gown and robe. He noticed that her face was delicately flushed and that she was also having trouble meeting his eyes, and he smiled. She was nervous.

Finally the champagne was gone. Nick sighed deeply and rose from his chair. He walked slowly around the table and reached for her hand. It felt warm and small and fragile. He closed his fingers around it and helped her stand. When he drew her into his arms, he felt a tremor pass through her body.

"Don't be afraid, Claire," he whispered.

"I'm not afraid."

He smiled into her eyes. Then he kissed her—a soft, coaxing kiss, and she slipped her arms around him, her mouth opening under his. Heat rushed through him, but he told himself to go slow, so he broke the kiss. He wanted this first time to be good for both of them and that meant he needed to stay in control. Taking her hand once more he led her into the bedroom.

Still holding her hand, he turned off the lamps until the only light in the room came from the leaping flames in the fireplace. Smiling down into her eyes, he began to untie the ribbons on her peignoir.

His body was already hard with desire, and as he helped her slip the peignoir off, his breathing quickened. The satin nightgown she wore was cut in a deep vee in the back, so that the line of her spine was clearly visible. With the firelight behind her, he could see the outline of her body through the gown.

She stood very still, waiting. Nick drew her into his arms, and with no hesitation, she lifted her face for his kiss.

This time the kiss was less gentle. This time he couldn't stop himself from driving his tongue into her mouth, and she accepted him fully. Soon his heart was thundering in his chest and he dragged his mouth from her lips. He wanted to kiss all of her. He started with her neck, tasting her as he went. His hands stroked her back, then dropped to her tight little bottom, and her skin felt like satin fire under his touch. When his mouth lowered to her breasts, and she shuddered, his own body throbbed in answer. He slid the thin straps of her gown off her shoulders, and the gown slithered down her body, pooling in a shimmery pile at her feet.

He looked at her. Her body was perfect. Long and slim and curved in all the right places, with a flat stomach and small, high breasts. He smiled. Her breasts had tightened, and he brushed his fingertips lightly over them, delighting in her sharply indrawn breath.

Then he lowered his head and took one hard nub into his mouth. Her fingers tangled in his hair, and when she gasped, Nick's blood pounded through his veins. After a long time, he backed up, drawing her with him, until he could sit on the bed. He spread his legs and pulled her closer, in between his thighs. Holding her bottom firmly, he kissed her stomach, above the line of her bikini panties. Then his hands slowly worked her panties down until he could see all of her. Only then did he untie his own robe, letting it fall away. Then he grasped her waist and lifted her, placing her beside him on the bed. The firelight danced over her body, and he bent over her. She touched his chest, raking her fingernails lightly over his nipples, and it was Nick's turn to gasp.

He took her hands and pulled them around his back, whispering, "Not yet." Then he began to kiss her again—kiss her and touch her—until she was almost whimpering with need. But each time she tried to do the same for him, he would say, "Not yet." He was determined he would not lose control, and he knew if he allowed her to do to him what he was doing to her, he would not be able to give her the pleasure he wanted to give her.

Finally, when she was slick and hot and ready, he guided her hand to him, and when her palm closed around him, he shuddered. But he only allowed himself a brief moment of pleasure before he opened her legs and slowly entered her, pushing as deep and hard as he could. When her welcoming warmth circled him, he could feel himself growing harder, and he began to move.

Soon she matched her movements to his, and her nails were digging into his back, and she was saying his name over and over again. Then, suddenly, her body began to convulse, and he could feel the spasms tearing through her body, and her cries mingled with his as his own release came quickly and fiercely and with a shuddering force that tore through him.

When they were finally spent, he wrapped his arms around her and rolled onto his back, bringing her with him. He was still inside her, and he liked the feeling. He held her face between his hands and kissed her.

"Claire, you are wonderful," he whispered. His heart was finally slowing down, and he could feel hers against his chest.

She looked at him, her eyes gleaming in the firelight. "You wouldn't let me do anything," she said softly. "Everything was for me."

He smiled. "I'm not complaining." He kissed her again. She was eminently kissable, he decided. He would kiss her often.

She didn't answer him, but it didn't worry Nick. He knew he'd given her great pleasure tonight, and he had certainly enjoyed making love to her. His smiled widened. And perhaps they'd made a baby. He really didn't need any more than that for himself. And even if it took awhile for Claire to conceive, that was all right, for he would enjoy making love to her often.

In fact, he might start again right now.

NINE

For Claire, the four days she and Nick spent at the St. Maurice were a carousel of sights and sounds, colors and scents. San Francisco was everything she had ever expected it to be. They did all the standard tourist things: Rode the cable cars from one end to another as they laughed and huddled together in the chill wind; climbed the hilly streets and were gasping for breath by the time they reached the top of the steep hills. Ambled through Fisherman's Wharf while they sampled the shrimp and clam chowder and crab cocktails sold at the open-air stands. Took the bay cruise past Alcatraz and Sausalito to Tiburon, and Claire's nose got sunburned. Walked the length of Grant Avenue—packed with hundreds of Chinese, both old and young—where Nick bought her a beautiful lapis bracelet and matching earrings and a fat little jade Buddha Claire instantly loved.

One evening Nick took her to the Far East Café, and Claire felt as if she were in the middle of a 1940s

Peter Lorre and Sidney Greenstreet movie. Their dapper Chinese waiter showed them into a private dining booth and drew the curtain, closing them in. They laughed together as Claire remarked that any minute she expected someone to slither into their booth with a secret message.

They strolled through Golden Gate Park and the Japanese Tea Garden, where Claire's senses were assaulted with the many colors and varieties of flowers; toured the Presidio; and spent one fascinating afternoon at the Palace of Fine Arts.

They sat on the wharf and ate sourdough rolls stuffed with spicy sausage and tangy mustard from the Boudin Bakery. They walked through throngs of tourists and gorged on creamy chocolate from Ghiardelli Square. They explored the North Beach area and chose flaky, rich cannoli from one of the many Italian bakeries.

But their most memorable evening was their last in the city. As they finished their preparations for the evening, Claire thought Nick looked impossibly handsome in his dark suit and paisley tie. And she felt impossibly sophisticated in her black silk cocktail suit—an outfit Natalie had insisted she buy one day when they'd gone shopping together. She had just finished her makeup and was dabbing scent behind her ears when Nick walked up behind her, smiling.

Their eyes met in the mirror, and something about the way he was looking at her caused Claire's breath to catch. She turned around slowly and he handed her a flat velvet box.

He smiled at the question in her eyes. "Open it."

Heart thumping, she snapped open the lid and saw the matching diamond necklace, bracelet, and earrings. She stared at them mesmerized. The stones sparkled like thousands of stars against the black satin lining. "Oh, Nick, I don't know what to say."

"Don't say anything." And then he drew her into his arms and kissed her—a long, deep, seductive kiss— and Claire forgot everything except the way she felt about him. She tightened her arms around him, pouring herself into her response. These past few days had meant so much to her. He meant so much to her. And she wanted him to feel the same way.

He was such a skillful lover. He did everything he knew would please her and arouse her. And she loved the attention, she did. But somehow it wasn't enough. Even if he wasn't in love with her, she needed to know she had some effect on his careful control. Just once, she thought, as she slipped her hands into his hair and kissed him passionately, just once, she wanted to make him lose that control and take her—fast and hard and hungry. Right now she could feel his heart racing against hers, and she wondered how he would react if she began undressing him, if she tried to seduce him. Would he forget their dinner reservation? Would he let her be the aggressor?

But she lost her nerve when he firmly disengaged her hands and broke the embrace. He laughed a bit self-consciously and said, "I've smeared your lipstick."

"I don't care."

"I do. I'm taking you someplace special tonight."

And so Claire, wanting to please him, telling herself to stop wishing for the impossible, repaired her lipstick and put on the diamonds. At first their weight and cool-ness felt strange, but as she turned from side to side and looked at them, at the way they caught the light and how they glittered against her skin, she decided she could get used to wearing them.

He took her to dinner at the Sheraton Palace Garden Court, and they drank champagne and listened to the string quartet and ate delicate scallops in the glass-roofed dining room. And Nick's eyes were filled with a look of pride.

"You look incredible," he told her as they left the restaurant. "Every man in the room is jealous of me."

And under the pleasure she felt at his obviously sincere compliment, Claire wondered if the pride of ownership was what he felt for her, if it was all he'd ever feel for her.

Later, when they were sipping after dinner drinks at the Top of the Mark and looking out over the spectacular view of the city, Nick leaned close and pressed his lips to her temple. "Let's go back to our room," he whispered.

And that night he made slow, very deliberate love to her, bringing her to the pinnacle of pleasure not once, but several times. And Claire fell asleep in his arms, telling herself it didn't matter that Nick was holding something back, that his lovemaking was as careful and planned as everything else he did.

After San Francisco, they spent four days in a low-slung, glass and cypress house in Monterey. Each morning Claire woke to the view of dazzling blue water and cloudless skies and to the sound of the seals who gathered on the sun-kissed rocks that dotted the shore. Here the tempo of their days changed, and they spent long, lazy days lying in the sun, doing nothing. Every afternoon they took a nap together in the big master bedroom, with the shutters closed against the bright sunlight and the ceiling fan whirring overhead.

And at night Nick devised a special pleasure for her. The house had a hot tub enclosed on the private deck in back and each night after they'd had a leisurely dinner, Nick would pour snifters of brandy for them and lead her onto the deck, where he'd slowly undress her, then himself.

They would slip naked into the steaming water, and Claire's heart would begin to thump and she would feel decadent and incredibly sexy as the water swirled around them, lapping at their bodies. Nick would kiss her for a long time; then, knowing exactly how each touch would make her feel, he would pull her onto his lap, tight up against him, and his hands would slide slowly around, and he would stroke her, finding every sensitive spot, every hidden crevice. Claire, who couldn't fight the weakness and desire he so expertly aroused, would lay her head back and give herself up to the erotic combination of the touch of his hands on her fevered skin and the heat of the water foaming around them and the powerful needs building inside her.

He seemed to delight in taking her as high as he could and keeping her there as long as possible. She would be weak with desire, trembling under his hands and mouth, and still he would withhold himself until she was almost incoherent with wanting him. And then he would take her, bringing her to a shuddering climax. Afterwards, he would stroke her gently until she was quiet. Then he would take her to bed and do it all over again.

She wondered, but was afraid to ask, what he was thinking and feeling. Was all this attention, all this pleasure-giving, a subconscious wish to dominate her so completely she would never have any will of her own? Or were his motives simpler? Did he simply want to make sure she was pregnant before their honeymoon was over?

After Monterey, they went up into the wine country and stayed at a beautiful inn near Calistoga. Claire loved the Napa Valley. She loved the sweet-smelling air and the sunshine and the rows and rows of grapes. She loved the verdant hills and the cloudless sky and the rustic feel to the towns and countryside. And she loved Nick. More and more each day. She felt drunk with her love and drunk with her sensual awareness of herself and her body and all the sensations and feelings Nick had evoked.

One morning, shortly after sunrise, with mist hanging low over the valley like a silvery veil, they took a ride in a hot air balloon. As the balloon floated over the vineyards, Claire's eyes met Nick's, and just for a moment, she saw something that confused her. What was it? she wondered. Tenderness? Sadness? Yearning? What?

But before she could identify it, the emotion, whatever it had been, disappeared, and afterwards, Claire wondered if she'd imagined it.

On the last night before they would return to San Francisco, then fly back to Houston, they had dinner at the inn, sitting in front of the open fireplace, drinking two bottles of wine and eating excellent Chateaubriand. Afterwards, they danced close together to the music of a talented trio of musicians who played old love songs with romantic feeling, and Claire could feel Nick's heart beating heavily against hers.

"Do you know the name of this song?" he murmured.

"It's from *The Umbrellas of Cherbourg*." She hummed along. "I don't remember the exact words, only that they're beautiful. Something about a thousand summers." She smiled softly. "The name of the song is *I Will Wait For You*."

He pulled her closer and a tremor tiptoed down Claire's spine. And when the lovely song ended, Nick clasped her firmly around the waist and led her toward the doorway and the elevator that would take them to their room. They were the only people in the elevator, and as soon as the doors slid shut, Nick's mouth covered hers. The kiss was hard and hungry and when the elevator dinged its arrival at the third floor, Claire's heart was filled with a wild, irrational hope. Because she'd seen something in Nick's eyes tonight—something primitive and untamed—something she'd never seen before.

Maybe tonight he would forget his technique. Maybe tonight they would be equal, a man and a woman who wanted each other too much to remember to do everything by the book. Claire hoped with all her heart this was so.

As soon as the door shut behind them, he was reaching behind her to unzip her dress, covering her face with restless kisses. Happiness began to build in Claire, along with the passion he was always able to arouse, as he forgot his finesse and his kisses became more fevered and demanding.

Then, so suddenly it was as if Claire had been doused with cold water, he drew back, almost shaking himself. She could see him slip into his mask of control, as if it were something tangible he could put on, like clothing. His hands lost their roughness, and once again, as he'd done so many times before, he started his slow seduction of her senses.

A sense of futility stole over Claire. Although she was not very experienced when it came to men, she knew instinctively that until Nick opened himself up, shared himself completely, allowed his feelings to rule rather than his brain, there was no hope that he would ever love her the way she wanted him to.

The way she loved him.

Two weeks later, in the middle of a meeting with his division managers, Nick was thinking about Claire. He stirred restlessly, only half hearing the report Ken Boudreaux was making. His fingers toyed with his Cross pen as vivid images of his wife played through his mind. What was wrong with him? he wondered. Ever since they'd returned to Houston, he hadn't been able to stop thinking about her. To stay away from her. No matter how many times he told himself he would not yield to the desire pounding through him, that he would simply make love to her for one purpose—to make a baby—he knew he was lying to himself. Each time he touched her, his control slipped another notch.

His fingers tightened around the pen. He couldn't afford these feelings. Hadn't counted on them. Didn't want them. Emotions like these disturbed the order of a person's life. Made them do irrational, stupid things. Made them weak. Made them vulnerable. *I won't allow myself to need her*.

He would fight this weakness. He would fight his feelings for her. Because, above all, he would not, could not, fall in love with her.

Something was wrong with Nick. He hadn't said anything, but in the weeks since they'd returned from San Francisco, Claire could sense a difference in him. At first, she'd hoped the difference meant he was falling in love with her, but she was afraid she'd been kidding herself.

He was still kind. Still considerate. Still attentive.

He continued to make love to her almost every night. But there was a wariness about him now, and she wasn't sure what had brought it about. Was he concerned because she wasn't pregnant yet? Was that it?

Something else bothered her, too. Every Saturday afternoon he went out, and he didn't tell her where he was going. That bothered Claire. She knew that under the terms of their marriage, he wasn't obligated to tell her everything, but still, it disturbed her that he was secretive. Because she knew he would be gone, she began visiting her mother on Saturday afternoons and made a point of telling him where she'd be. She thought he would respond in kind. But he never did, just said, "Have a nice visit."

Finally, one Saturday early in August, she confronted him. She was in the sunroom relaxing with a book when he walked in and casually said, "I'm going out for a few hours. I'll see you later."

She laid her book down. He was dressed casually in white shorts, white athletic shoes, and a royal blue cotton shirt that matched his eyes. "Where are you going, Nick?"

For a minute she thought he wasn't going to answer. A thoughtful look crossed his face, and his blue eyes studied her. "The Buffalo Children's Home."

His answer was so entirely unexpected, Claire didn't say anything for a minute. Then she smiled. "Would you take me with you?"

Buffalo Children's Home sat on the top of a gently sloped hill on the banks of Buffalo Bayou near downtown Houston. It had originally been the home of a man who had made a fortune in the oil fields of West Texas and had wanted a mansion to prove he was one of the elite. He had subsequently lost his fortune because of lousy judgment at the gaming tables and in his choice of women. A group of civic-minded citizens had banded together to buy the opulent home and turned it into a children's shelter. Through the years the home had become one of Houston's landmarks, both in real estate and as an instrument for raising social consciousness.

As Claire walked beside Nick through the heavy oak doors and into the large marble-floored entryway with its twenty-foot ceiling graced by an ornate chandelier, she remembered all the stories she'd read about the home and wondered why she'd never visited before. The receptionist, a petite redhead, smiled as they approached.

"Hello, Mr. Callahan."

"Hello, Dawn." He put his arm loosely around Claire's waist. "This is my wife."

The redhead grinned. A few minutes later, they were following her bouncy figure down a long hallway which led to the rear of the house and into an enormous room that was brightly lit from a solid wall of long windows filled with hanging baskets of ferns and flowers.

A group of children ranging in age from about six to fourteen were laughing and talking, and when they saw Nick, they immediately surrounded him. Within minutes, he was sitting in the middle of the floor with the kids on all sides. His dark hair was no longer perfectly combed and a thick lock fell over his forehead, giving him a little-boy look that was completely at odds with the powerful, in-charge persona he usually wore.

Nick looked at her and smiled. "This is Claire, guys. I told you about her. Claire, these are my buddies." He pointed to a good-looking boy of about ten with ink-black hair and large brown eyes. "This is Ricardo, the star pitcher of the softball team." Next came a girl with protruding teeth and a shy smile. "This is Sarah. She plays left field." One by one he pointed them out: Jeff, Jimmy, Shari, Lorraine, Valerie, James, Doug, David, Allison, Elizabeth, Lisa, Joey, Jason. After each name, he added the position they played on the team. "And this young lady is Brigette, our cheerleader," he finished with a grin and a wink.

"Cheerleader?" Claire said, mind whirling from his rapid-fire introductions.

"Somebody has to do it," said the tall, animated girl with long, golden-brown hair and dancing blue eyes. She was about thirteen and pretty enough to be a model. Claire warmed to her instantly.

"Nick helps our coach," piped up a stocky-looking black boy with a scarred face and sweet smile. Claire couldn't remember his name. "When he can make it."

"We're the Callahan's Commanders," boasted another boy.

" 'Cause we're always in command," said one of the girls.

"Like Nick," said the one he'd called Sarah, grinning at Nick with a gap-toothed smile.

"That's enough bragging," Nick said, "let's hear the weekly report." Claire sat on a chair near the fringes of the group where she could watch.

"Lisa got two demerits," said a skinny blond boy, " 'cause she sassed Mrs. Ford."

Nick shook his head at Lisa, a small, dark girl who didn't look the least bit sorry for her lapse. "Got anything to say for yourself, Lisa?"

"She made me mad," Lisa said.

"That's what you always say," Nick said dryly. "What did I tell you about that?"

Lisa shrugged her shoulders, and Claire wanted to laugh at the flash of defiance in her eyes. None of Nick Callahan's adversaries openly defied him, but here was this tiny girl of about twelve who didn't seem the least bit intimidated by him.

"Didn't I tell you to count to ten and think before you answer back?" Nick persisted.

"Yeah." Lisa rolled her eyes.

"Then why don't you do it?"

Another shrug. "I try, but she says such dumb things sometimes, and I . . . well, I can't stand it."

Sympathy for Nick caused Claire to smother a smile. Obviously Lisa was not a child who would be easily molded into any pattern she didn't fit. "A kid after my own heart," he muttered under his breath, "who doesn't easily suffer fools."

Claire watched in fascination as Nick talked to the kids about their week, praising them for their small victories and gently chiding them for their transgressions.

He obviously knew the children well. It was evident that he came here often.

Later, they moved upstairs to the nursery and Nick picked up a little redheaded boy of about eighteen months whose right arm was in a cast, putting him on his knee and cuddling him.

A woman named Norma explained to Claire that Scotty, the name they'd given the boy, had been abandoned two weeks earlier, and that examinations had revealed long-term child abuse. Claire blinked back tears. How could anyone abuse a child? she wondered. When she and Nick had a child she'd cherish it and love it and thank God every day for giving it to her.

After they once again returned to the first floor, Claire watched and listened as Nick talked to Paul

Civic, the director of the home, and his wife, Gerri. The three of them went over the books and talked about the new roof the home needed. From Nick's questions Claire realized he was intimately aware of all aspects of the running of the home, from its financial situation to the day-to-day work involved in an undertaking of this magnitude.

By the time she and Nick walked outside, Claire's concept of who and what her husband was had taken on another dimension. She'd always known about his aggressive side, the part of him that ruthlessly manipulated people—including her—using any and all weaknesses to his advantage. She'd also seen his softer side, one that was compassionate and caring, even though he exposed that side less often. And now today she'd seen something even deeper, a part of him that needed to give and receive love, a part of him that was vulnerable and lonely, a secret part of him that until now she had been afraid did not exist. Hope swelled her heart.

"Aren't they great kids?" he asked, a smile lighting his eyes. They stood just outside the front door.

There was a lump in Claire's throat as she nodded, suddenly assailed by longing as she remembered the feel of Scotty's soft skin when she'd kissed his cheek before they left. She wanted so much to give Nick a son like Scotty.

"I'm glad you came today. I wanted to tell you about the kids, but before we were married I was afraid you'd think I was trying to make myself look good. And afterwards, well, I wasn't sure how you'd feel."

"I don't understand."

"Let's go sit over there," he suggested, pointing to a bench on the front lawn.

When they were seated side by side with his arm

draped casually over the back of the bench, he stared off into the distance, where Claire could see the downtown skyline just beyond the banks of the bayou. A jet passed overhead, a small splash of silver against the blue sky. A few feet away, a cardinal sat perched on a low hanging branch of an ancient oak tree. The air was hot and still.

"The first time I visited the home, it was with the intention of adopting one of the kids. But I changed my mind after I'd been here several times."

"Why?"

"Because by the time I knew the kids well enough to know which one I might want to adopt, I couldn't choose just one. So I decided to adopt them all. To come here as many times a week as I could manage."

Claire's eyes misted. His voice had taken on a gruffness that told her how deeply he felt about the children.

"I know what it's like to feel unwanted. I didn't want any of the kids to feel that way. At least not because of me."

"Tell me about it," she said gently, knowing they were on the verge of something—a line, a barrier, something. She wasn't sure what it was; she only knew that if she could get him to cross it, things would be different between them.

He turned and his eyes were incredibly blue in the sunlight. He studied her for a long time. "Not now. Maybe I'll tell you about it another time."

She wanted so desperately to tell him what she was feeling, but if he persisted in keeping this distance between them, she couldn't.

"I'm doing my damnedest to find good homes for every single one of these kids," he said. "Do you think I'm doing the right thing?'' There was a note of uncertainty in his voice.

Impulsively, Claire reached up and smoothed back his stray lock of hair, then she let her hand slide down to touch his cheek. Their eyes met again, and Claire's heart thudded up into her throat. ''Yes,'' she said softly. ''I think you're doing the right thing.''

He touched her hand, holding it against his cheek. As his warm, strong fingers closed around hers, she could feel the heat transfer itself from him, a connection of flesh that caused a fine tremor to pulse through her. A fierce longing consumed her.

Then the moment passed. He released her hand and said, ''It's getting late. We'd better be going. We're due at the MacAllisters' at seven.''

That night, when they made love, Claire felt closer to him than she'd ever felt before. She felt she was making progress, when, during his climax, he called her name, and there was desperation in the sound. But he was still holding something back.

Afterwards, when he was sleeping soundly beside her, one arm thrown over her stomach, Claire lay in the darkness, happiness humming through her.

She was positive that tonight she had conceived and was carrying Nick's baby inside.

TEN

Claire's heart sank at the first twinge of cramps. Why? She asked herself yet again. She and Nick had been married for almost four months now. And each month, on the dot of the 28th day, her period would start.

Why couldn't she get pregnant? The one thing Nick wanted from her, she still hadn't been able to give him. And he had given her so much.

Claire's thoughts turned to Kitty. From the day of their wedding, Nick had been wonderful with her mother. If Claire wanted to visit her in the evening, he always accompanied her. In fact, they had visited Pinehaven the previous evening.

"You don't have to go with me," she had protested. "I know you're tired." She was worried. Lately he'd seemed preoccupied. She wondered if his preoccupation had anything to do with her inability to get pregnant.

He smiled down at her. "I want to." He touched her cheek with his fingertips. "I don't like you going

157

to the nursing home at night alone. Besides, I enjoy Kitty.''

Claire swallowed against the sudden lump in her throat. When he was thoughtful and protective, she loved him so much it was almost a physical pain. At that moment, she would have given anything, anything at all, to hear him say he loved her.

She smiled wryly. She was such a fool.

Sighing, she decided that if she still wasn't pregnant next month she would go back to the doctor. Perhaps there was something she could do that she wasn't doing. Maybe she and Nick were making love too often.

She decided to call Peachey and see if she'd like to go to the Buffalo Children's Home with her that afternoon. Going there would certainly take her mind off her own problems.

"Oh, sugar, I wish I could, but I have an appointment with my accountant. Quarterly taxes are due in three weeks, and he says it's time we had a talk." Peachey chuckled, the sound warm and friendly, making Claire smile. "He's mad at me. Says I have no sense when it comes to money."

Claire knew that wasn't true at all. Peachey was extremely sensible about her finances. "I never see you anymore," she said. "When are you coming to dinner?"

"How about this weekend?"

"It's a date. Saturday night?"

"Saturday night it is."

"Will you bring a date?"

"Nope. I've sworn off men for a while."

Now it was Claire's turn to chuckle. "Would you mind if I asked Tim Sutherland to come then?"

"You mean that tight-assed lawyer-right-hand-man of Nick's? I thought you couldn't stand him."

"Well, I've gotten to know him better, and he's really quite nice." Claire was surprised herself. She hadn't expected to like Tim, but after the first few times they'd been together, his stiffness and suspicion gradually faded, and now she found she enjoyed his company. He was actually very nice and he was devoted to Nick. Claire mentally laughed at herself. She already felt a fierce loyalty to Nick, so how could she dislike Tim, who obviously felt the same way?

"Okay. See you about seven on Saturday."

After she and Peachey concluded their conversation, Claire showered and dressed. One of the many pleasures of her new life as the wife of Nick Callahan was her extensive wardrobe, a wardrobe that Nick insisted she constantly add to. Today, even though it was late September, the weather forecast was for hot temperatures, in the high eighties with high humidity, so Claire chose a cool-looking aquamarine linen sundress. Now that she spent so much time lounging around the pool, her legs were nicely tanned, so she left them bare, slipping them into matching turquoise sandals. She was letting her hair grow longer in response to a comment of Nick's, so she swept her hair back from her face with a headband.

By ten o'clock she was ready to face the world and after telling Mrs. Swift, the full-time housekeeper who had been with Nick for years, where she was going and when she'd be back, Claire walked out to the six-car garage where her shining green Mercedes sat neatly between Nick's blue Porsche and red Maserati. She smiled. He'd taken the Lotus today.

He was like a kid sometimes, she thought, as she

carefully backed the beautiful car out of the garage, then lowered the automatic door with her hand control. He loved expensive toys, and he loved giving her toys to play with, too. This car was one, but Claire had to admit she loved it. She ran her hand possessively against the Italian calfskin leather seat, smelled the new-car smell it still held, and sighed happily. She'd never thought she would own a car like this one.

Nick also showered her with jewelry. Almost every week, something new would be sitting beside her dinner plate in a velvet box. At first she'd protested.

"Nick. You've already given me this magnificent ring." She held up her hand to wave her engagement ring at him. "And the pearls." She fingered the warm stones at her throat. "And the diamond necklace and bracelet and earrings. That's enough for any woman."

"Nonsense. I've only just started." His eyes, deep as the ocean and just as blue, rested softly on her face.

Her jewelry box, which had soon overflowed and been supplemented by the wall safe in their bedroom, now contained an exquisite emerald ring surrounded by diamonds, an enormous ruby ring with a matching pendant and earrings, a starburst ring with tiny sapphires on each point and a matching starburst pendant, an evening watch studded with diamonds and pearls, a long rope of black pearls and matching earrings, several thick gold necklaces, a half dozen gold bracelets, a diamond tennis bracelet, and dozens of gold earrings, both big and small.

The array was at first bewildering, but Claire found it didn't take her long to get used to receiving the gifts. In fact, she was a little disgusted with herself because she loved being given all these beautiful things. She could see how money could corrupt a person, because its power was seductive.

Money, she had discovered, could ease almost anything. Make any difficult chore simple. Reduce any problem to the manageable. Soothe disturbances and smooth a path that was rocky. Married to Nick, the tempo of her life had gone from uneven and uncertain to smooth and sheltered. She gardened, she shopped, she read, she visited the children at Buffalo Children's Home—taking special pleasure in her growing closeness to Brigette, the enchanting teenager she'd met the first day, and she spent hours at Pinehaven with Kitty.

An hour later, as she sat at the children's home and talked to Brigette, her thoughts once more turned to Nick. Being around the children always reminded her of why Nick had married her.

And later, as she drove home again, she was still thinking about him. She knew he watched the calendar as closely as she did, and she knew there would be a question in his eyes tonight. And once more, he would be disappointed.

Nick tried not to let his disappointment show, but he felt it like a body blow. Why? he asked himself. What's wrong with us? Surely, after four months of lovemaking, they should have been able to conceive a baby.

But he could see Claire's eyes were cloudy with her own disappointment, so he forced himself to laugh lightly and draw her into his arms. They were in the tower room, her favorite place, where she waited for him each evening. They had fallen into the habit of sharing a drink before dinner, and he would tell her about his day, loosening his tie and kicking off his shoes. She would be curled up on one end of the couch, turned toward him, and she would listen quietly and he would feel all the cares of the day slipping from his shoulders.

Now he gently removed the glass she was holding from her fingers and set it on the coffee table in front of them, then he kissed her, feeling her immediate response. He closed his eyes, inhaling her scent, and deepened the kiss. She felt so good in his arms. He liked holding her. He loved kissing her. He loved . . . He broke off the thought.

The half-formed thought shook his equilibrium, and he reluctantly broke the kiss. But he couldn't resist comforting her, and he smoothed his palms over her satiny cheeks, rubbing his thumbs over the corners of her soft mouth. "Don't worry, Claire. It'll happen when it's meant to happen. We have a lot of time." He smiled to show her he meant what he'd just said. And he did. They *did* have a lot of time. Years, in, fact. Men had fathered children into their sixties, even their seventies. Forty-two wasn't *that* old.

Something heavy knotted inside him as he thought about the years he had ahead of him. Years of making love to Claire. Years of touching her, holding her, sharing those shattering peaks of pleasure with her. Years of talking to her, watching her, protecting her. Years of giving her presents, of seeing her eyes light up, of making her happy.

He took her hands in his, held them firmly, and forced a lighthearted tone into his voice. "We'll just have to keep trying until we get it right."

And then he kissed her again.

She should always wear green, Nick decided as he watched Claire get ready Saturday night. Her dress was a long column of jade silk, slit up the back to give a tantalizing view of slim, elegant legs. Its cummberbund was made of the same material, gathered into tight folds and studded with tiny winking rhinestones. Her hair, long and thick, was swept back from her ears by diamond-studded combs, and she wore matching diamond earrings. She was made to wear jewels, he thought with satisfaction.

She smiled as she turned from her mirror.

She was incredibly beautiful, he thought.

Later, as they sat with their guests over coffee and lemon tarts, Nick watched the play of candlelight across her delicate features. She seemed to shimmer tonight, obviously enjoying herself and the company of their friends. Peachey, a woman Nick had liked from the first moment he'd met her, looked striking in fire-engine red, her dark, dramatic beauty a perfect complement to Claire's fair incandescence.

And Tim. Nick's attention settled on his friend. Tim had certainly changed his attitude toward Claire. Nick watched him now as he basked in Claire's smiling attention. He said something to her, something low that Nick didn't catch because Peachey was talking to him and he was listening to her while watching Tim, and Nick saw the way Claire tilted her head up and laughed—the sound full-throated and rich.

He saw the way Tim watched her, and something he tightened in his gut as he saw Tim's reaction to Claire's amusement, the way his mouth tipped up at the corners, the warmth in his eyes, the faint flush on his face, the almost possessive way he leaned toward her. Nick could feel his muscles tensing, and all thought was wiped out of his mind except one.

Tim was in love with Claire.

Nick knew it, knew it as surely as he knew his own name. Anger and something else, something hot and painful, constricted his chest. Damn it all. His best friend, the man he counted on, the one person he thought he could trust, was in love with his wife!

Nick had been so quiet for the past hour. Claire watched him covertly and wondered why. He had seemed to be having a good time for most of the evening, and then, suddenly, when they were just finishing their dessert, his whole demeanor had changed. He had become silent and brooding, his blue eyes darkening, his mouth tightening.

Claire, who had been having such a good time, began to count the minutes until Peachey and Tim would go home. But neither of them seemed inclined to go. Neither of them even seemed to notice Nick's withdrawal. They laughed and talked, drawing her into the conversation and ignoring Nick's black mood. But Claire was all too aware of him sitting there, eyes darkened to indigo, hands cradling his brandy glass.

Finally Peachey stood up. "Gotta go, sugar," she said.

"Yes," Tim agreed. "It's late."

Claire and Nick walked them to the front door, and the two women hugged. Then Tim took her hands and smiled. "Thank you, Claire. It was a lovely evening."

"I'm glad you could come," she said, smiling up into his warm brown eyes. He bent to kiss her cheek, and over his shoulder she saw the scowl on Nick's face. Her heart bumped painfully when she realized he was very angry. But why? she wondered. What had happened to make him so furious? Had she done something?

When they were finally alone, Claire walked into the

dining room. She leaned over the table to blow out the candles. Silently, Nick came up behind her. He gripped her upper arm, turned her around.

The look in his eyes disturbed her, but she didn't intend to let him know it. "I thought I'd just clear these dishes away."

"Leave them." His voice was edged with steel.

"But—"

"That's what Lucille and Mrs. Swift get paid to do." His eyes glittered in the semi-darkness, and Claire swallowed. "Come to bed."

Why? Because that's what I get paid to do? Claire was ashamed of the thought, but it hammered at the back of her mind. His hand was not gentle as he tugged her along behind him, up the wide staircase to the second floor, down the long hallway into their private wing, where he shut the double doors that closed off the wing firmly behind him.

He began to undress, his mouth, his entire body set in stern, uncompromising lines.

Silently, Claire removed her earrings, then her other jewelry. As she walked unhurriedly to the dressing area, she unfastened her cummerbund. While she continued undressing, she heard him moving about the bedroom, then the half dozen speakers spread throughout their private wing came alive with sound.

Nick always played music at night. Claire had come to expect it and enjoy it, knowing exactly what his mood was by his selection.

She shivered. Tonight Beethoven's "Fifth Symphony" vibrated through the rooms, its power and strength heightening her tension. Drawing on a teal satin nightgown, she delayed the moment when she'd have to walk out into the bedroom and face him.

But finally she could delay no longer.

Wearing only the bottoms of dark silk pajamas, Nick stood in the middle of the room, legs slightly spread apart, eyes narrowed as they swept her from head to foot.

Breathing faster than she'd have liked, Claire attempted a casual smile. "It was a nice evening, wasn't it?"

"I'm sure *you* enjoyed it," he said tightly.

Claire frowned. "What's that remark supposed to mean?"

One eyebrow lifted. "Don't play dumb, Claire. It doesn't suit you."

Honestly bewildered, she moved toward him, touched his arm. "Please, Nick. Don't play games with me. I really have no earthly idea what you're talking about."

"I'm talking about the way you flirted with Tim tonight, the way you've been leading him on. That's what I'm talking about."

Astonishment and disbelief collided in Claire's mind. Her mouth dropped open. For a moment, she was so stunned, she couldn't think of a single thing to say.

He walked stiffly to the bed, removed his pajama bottoms, letting them slide to the floor, then naked, slipped between the sheets and leaned back against the headboard. Chest taut, eyes darkly gleaming, the music swelling around them, he said, "Take that nightgown off and come here."

Trembling with a combination of anger and fear and the growing realization that he was jealous, jealous of Tim, jealous of Tim's attentions to her, and the bewildering array of emotions that knowledge stirred, Claire did as she was told.

When she joined him in the bed, he moved over her,

and just before he took her mouth, he said, "You belong to me, Claire. Don't ever forget that. And I don't share what belongs to me."

Then, with the drums and horns and strings thundering around them, he took the rest of her.

October came and went, and still Claire wasn't pregnant. She put off going to the doctor. She was afraid the doctor would find something wrong with her, and like an ostrich, she preferred to bury her head in the sand.

But when, just after Thanksgiving, her period rolled around again, she knew she could put off her visit no longer. So she called Dr. Ardale and made an appointment for the following week.

Her relationship with Nick had changed after the night he'd been so angry with her over Tim. He was still considerate, still generous, but the closeness she had felt them beginning to share had disappeared. Once more, he was holding himself back from her, but this time it wasn't in the form of his lovemaking.

No, Claire thought, shivering as she remembered the fiery quality of his lovemaking the past five weeks. Nick was not holding back there. He was fierce and demanding and dominating. He was everything Claire had ever hoped he would be, but all the tenderness was gone.

Claire didn't know how to cope with this new side of him. She wished she could believe he was acting like this because he loved her, but unfortunately, she didn't think love was the reason. She thought he was simply showing her that she was his possession, and that he would always be the one to set the rules. She thought he had really meant what he'd said when he told her she belonged to him, that he didn't share what was his.

In other words, she was bought and paid for.

On some level, Claire understood his feelings, even if it hurt to have him behave this way. On another level, she was confused and unhappy, wondering if this unnatural bargain of theirs would work after all.

If only she could give him a child. Maybe then he could let go of his mistrust. Maybe then he could let himself believe in her. Believe in them. Maybe then he could love her.

"Mrs. Callahan, there is not one thing wrong with you," Dr. Ardale declared kindly, blue eyes twinkling behind thick glasses. "You are healthy, normal, and fertile, as far as I can tell. All your tests are fine. There's no reason you shouldn't have as many children as you want."

Relief washed over Claire. Thank God, she thought.

"Perhaps you're trying too hard. I've seen the same phenomena in many patients. Once they relax, they conceive. Forget about getting pregnant. That's my best advice."

That night, when she told Nick what the doctor had said, he had a thoughtful look in his eyes. He didn't come up to bed when she did, either. He stayed in his study until very late. Claire knew what time he eventually did come to bed. It was after two. But she pretended to be asleep. It was obvious he didn't want to make love to her.

The next day he told her he had to go to Boston on business. "I'll be back in three or four days. I'll call you."

While he was gone she spent more time with Kitty.

She was a little worried about her mother, who seemed rundown and listless. On the last afternoon before Nick's return, Claire went to the nursing home and found her mother in bed. Her mother hated being in bed, and Claire knew if she were there, she must really be feeling ill. Kitty's face looked flushed and her eyes were glazed.

"Are you sick, Mom?" Claire laid her palm against her mother's forehead. It felt hot, too hot.

"What's wrong with her?" she asked the nurse on duty.

"Now, don't worry, Mrs. Callahan. She's just got a cold. She complained about her chest hurting last night."

Claire frowned. She hated that patronizing tone some nurses and doctors adopted. She wasn't stupid and she didn't worry needlessly. Despite what the nurse said, she didn't like the look of Kitty's eyes.

"She'll be fine," the nurse insisted.

But Claire couldn't stop worrying, and even Nick's homecoming the next day couldn't keep her mind from her mother for long.

At dinner he mentioned her preoccupation. "Is something wrong?"

Her eyes met his. She sighed. "I'm worried about my mother. She's sick." She quickly explained Kitty's condition. "When I was there today, I had a chance to talk to Dr. Phillips and he finally admitted he's worried about pneumonia."

Nick frowned. "Shouldn't she be in the hospital?"

"I asked him that and he assured me that if her condition warrants a move, she'll be moved." Claire sighed. "He's a good doctor. I think he'll watch her closely."

Nick didn't say anything else, but his eyes were thoughtful. Later, as they were preparing for bed, he said, "I'll call tomorrow and talk to Dr. Phillips myself, Claire."

A warm rush of gratitude filled her heart. "Thank you. That will make me feel a lot better."

Still later, as they lay in bed together, he said, "I went to see a specialist while I was in Boston."

Claire's heart jumped in alarm. "What's wrong?"

"Don't worry. There's nothing wrong . . ." He hesitated, then said, "I wanted assurance that I wasn't sterile."

Sterile! Had he been worried that it was his fault she hadn't conceived?

"But all the tests showed everything's normal." He tightened his arms around her. "So neither one of us needs to worry about your not getting pregnant yet. The specialist agreed with Dr. Ardale. He said we're worrying about it too much."

That night, Claire fell asleep more lighthearted than she'd felt in weeks, secure in the knowledge that Nick would take care of everything.

Two days later Kitty was moved to the hospital. She was diagnosed with double pneumonia. For a few days after she'd been admitted, her condition remained stable but serious. Then, abruptly, several complications developed, among them abseses on both lungs and pleurisy.

Nick called his office and told Wanda to cancel all his appointments. "I'll be here at the hospital if you need me," he said.

He could see how worried Claire was. Her face was pale and strained. For hours they sat together outside

Kitty's room. She had been moved into intensive care, and they were permitted to see her for five minutes every hour.

After forty-six straight hours during which Claire refused to leave her mother, Nick was still at her side. He did everything he could to alleviate her burden: he talked to the doctors, he insisted she eat, he paid for a room down the hall from the waiting room and forced Claire to lie down. She didn't sleep, but she did rest.

Finally, at five o'clock that afternoon, Kitty's condition improved slightly, and her doctor came out to talk with Claire and Nick.

"She's doing better," he said. He glanced at Claire, then directed his remark to Nick. "Why don't you take your wife home, Mr. Callahan? Both of you could use a good night's sleep. Come back in the morning."

"I don't want to leave," Claire said.

Nick hated to pressure her, but he could see that she wasn't going to last much longer. She was devoid of color except for dark smudges beneath her eyes. He gave the doctor a meaningful look. The doctor nodded slightly.

"Mrs. Callahan, I promise I will phone you if anything changes."

"But—"

"Go home, get some rest."

"Nick?" She looked up.

Nick's chest tightened when he saw the frightened expression in Claire's eyes. "It'll be okay," he promised. He put his arm around her waist, and when she laid her head against his shoulder, he hoped he was right.

Where was it? She had to find it. It was somewhere, somewhere in the fog. Claire tried to take a step, but the thick fog swirled around her, and when she tried to escape its creeping tendrils, her legs wouldn't work. She cried out as the fog crept closer. "No, no, I have to go. I have to." Her heart pounded in fear. She felt so helpless. Panic was beginning to set in.

Someone was talking softly. Someone held her shoulders. "Claire, it's okay. You were dreaming. You're okay."

Nick. She fell back against the pillows and opened her eyes. The bedroom was dark except for the soft glow of the lamp in their adjoining sitting room.

Claire shuddered. "Wh . . . what time is it?"

Nick slipped his arm around her and pulled her close. His body felt warm and safe. His lips nuzzled her temple. "It's four-thirty."

Four-thirty. She'd been dreaming she had to go somewhere, but she wasn't able to move. She could still taste the fear when she'd realized she was helpless. She shivered again.

"Were you dreaming about your mother?"

"No . . . at least I don't think so . . . I . . . felt as if I'd lost something, as if I had to find it, but I was helpless. I couldn't make my legs move. I was so afraid."

His arms tightened. "Well, the dream's over. You're safe here with me, darling."

Claire lay very still. *Darling.* He'd called her darling. She turned her head toward him. "Nick," she whispered, but the whisper was cut off as his lips met hers.

He made love to her with sweetness and tenderness and a giving of himself that made Claire feel warm and comforted and protected. And when they came together in a stunning climax, she clung to him.

Afterward, she dozed off to sleep once more, only waking when she heard Nick talking in low tones.

She sat up sleepily. Muted sunlight filled the bedroom. Nick stood with his back to her as he spoke softly into the bedside phone. She smiled. He'd been away from his office for nearly three days.

But when he turned around and she saw his face, she went cold inside. His eyes never leaving her face, he walked around the bed. "Claire . . ."

She knew. She knew even before he spoke.

"Claire, darling, I'm so sorry." He sat on her side of the bed and drew her into his arms.

ELEVEN

No! Claire's mind screamed a denial. *No!* She stared at Nick. "How . . . what happened?"

"She just gave up. Quit fighting. They tried everything, but they couldn't save her."

"Mom," Claire whispered. Tears gushed from her eyes as her body shook uncontrollably. Nick's arms held her tightly, his hands stroked her hair and her back.

Images of her mother swirled through her mind. Kitty baking peanut butter cookies. Kitty singing in the kitchen, her high, clear voice floating in the air. Kitty playing the piano. Kitty posing in front of the mirror in her bedroom, trying on one dress after another. Kitty bringing Claire hot tea and cinnamon toast when Claire was home with a bad cold.

Her mother was only fifty-three years old. How could she be dead?

Mom, Mom. Don't leave me. Please don't leave me.

The one person who had always thought Claire was

perfect was gone. Claire felt as if the anchor that had kept her securely fastened to the world had slipped, and now she was cartwheeling through space with nothing to hold on to.

All the tears Claire hadn't shed over the past six years, she shed now. She felt as if she'd never be able to stop crying. And the whole time, Nick held her and whispered comforting words. Finally, when her tears had subsided he gently helped her from the bed.

"Why don't you take a hot bath, and I'll call your aunt and uncle and Peachey," he said. He squeezed her hands.

Claire nodded numbly. Her head throbbed and her eyes felt grainy. She heard him making the calls while she soaked in the hot water, but her brain refused to function the way it normally did. She soaped herself, rinsed, dried herself, began to dress—but all the while her mind was divorced from her physical activity. All she could think about was Kitty. Now her mother would never be the person Claire remembered. Kitty's life was over, and Claire would never see her again.

Claire sat at her dressing table and stared at herself in the mirror. The haunted face staring back at her didn't look like anyone she knew. She shivered against the thought that refused to disappear. Lowering her head onto her arms, she closed her eyes.

Her mother was dead.

Now there was no one left who loved Claire unconditionally.

No one.

Aunt Susan and Uncle Dale and Peachey had all come and gone again. Claire moved through the day like a sleepwalker. She heard the words people said, but they had no real meaning. When Nick gave her two pills to take, saying, "Claire, take these. Then try to get some rest."

"I want to go see my mother," she said.

"Later. We can't see her until later today." He bent and kissed her cheek. "Please, darling. Lie down. You're going to need your strength in the next couple of days."

Wearily, she succumbed. She took the pills, then lay on the bed and tried to sleep. Anything to escape her thoughts. Even Nick's tenderness and his continued use of the endearment darling failed to bring her comfort. She wasn't sure how much time had passed, but when she couldn't sleep, she headed for the tower room, a place she had come to think of as her refuge.

Later that afternoon, just as the shadows began to lengthen, Claire heard the low rumble of voices in Nick's study downstairs. She shook off the fog of half-sleep and rose from the loveseat. She recognized Tim's voice. She walked toward the stairway, actually had one foot on the top rung when Tim's voice stopped her.

"Will her mother's death affect your arrangement with Claire?"

Suddenly her mind was clear of all cobwebs, and she froze.

Nick's reply was clear and devoid of emotion. "Why should it? I still want a child. Even though Kitty is dead, Claire won't back out on our agreement."

"What if she never gets pregnant? What then?" Tim said.

A cold lump settled into Claire's breast. The same question had been haunting her for months. The sense of loss and loneliness that had been so overwhelming throughout the long, terrible day settled over her shoulders like a cloak of armor—heavy and inescapable. On top of losing Kitty, would she also lose Nick? Whether or not he loved her, she loved him, and life without him didn't bear thinking about.

But was she being fair to him? If she couldn't conceive a child for him, was it fair to keep him shackled to her out of some sense of fair play? Shouldn't she offer to give him a divorce so that he could find someone else—someone who *could* give him a child?

Claire closed her eyes against the pain that gripped her. A life without Kitty. Without Nick. Without love.

Please, God. Let me be pregnant now. Let last night's lovemaking result in a child. A little Kitty who can bear her grandmother's name. Someone I can love who will love me back. Please, God. I want a baby so badly—for me and for Nick.

Three days later, Claire stood at the graveside and watched as the minister read a final prayer before the casket was lowered into the ground. It was only mid-December, but overnight a cold front had moved in and the day was overcast and chilly with a forecast of rain. She shivered although she wore her full-length ranch mink. She felt numb. The events of the past days—Kitty's death, the hours at the funeral home, the scores of flowers, many of them from Nick's business acquaintances and friends, the cards and calls, the whole ritual of death—had kept her moving, but inside she felt hollow, with an emptiness that frightened her, and two thoughts churned over and over in her mind.

Her mother was gone.

And if she couldn't conceive a child for him, she would lose her husband, too.

* * *

That night, as Nick drew her into his arms, the emptiness was so vast she felt devoid of all feeling. And for the first time in their marriage, she said, "Not tonight," and rolled away from him. Then she lay for hours with her eyes open.

December 18th. It was one week before Christmas. Ten more days to wait. She and Nick hadn't made love since the night of Kitty's death. Claire didn't know why, but in some twisted way, she felt she didn't deserve the comfort of his arms and the pleasure he gave her. She was either pregnant now or she never would be. And if she never would be, she'd better get used to going without his lovemaking.

Christmas Day. It was a blur of images. Nick tried so hard, but nothing he said or did made Claire feel alive. They kept their celebration small because of Claire's bereavement—just Peachey and Tim and Claire's aunt and uncle—and Claire tried to take part, tried to enjoy the day, but even Nick's gift—an exquisite jewel-incrusted music box that played "I Will Wait For You," which Claire knew was Nick's reminder of their honeymoon—failed to give her joy or hope. Inside of her, she could feel a clock ticking, a relentless countdown. Three more days, it said. Three more days.

But she didn't have to wait that long.

The day after Christmas, two days ahead of her normal cycle, Claire felt the dull ache of cramps beginning.

Claire took a deep breath, raised her fist, and knocked on the door of Nick's study.

"Come in," he called.

She opened the door, and he looked up and smiled.

"Hi. Why'd you knock? You know you're always welcome in here." He stood, and when she walked toward him, he placed his hands on her upper arms and leaned and kissed her cheek. "Feeling better after your nap?" he asked, and she could see the concern in his eyes.

Claire held herself stiffly. Pain suffused her, but she couldn't allow herself to give in to it. All night she'd lain sleepless. She hadn't told Nick about this latest disappointment. And since he'd been treating her very gently since Kitty's death, he didn't try to force her to make love. When he touched her shoulder and she shook her head, he didn't push her.

So he didn't know. Yet.

She drew back from him. Met his eyes. She would miss him so much. But last night, during those long, sleepless hours, she'd faced the truth.

Her mother was gone.

Nick didn't love her.

And she couldn't conceive a child.

She had nothing to offer her husband. So she had to release him. And she had to do it in such a way that he wouldn't feel guilty or pity her. She had to make him angry. She had to make him feel wronged. She had to make him despise her.

She lifted her chin. "There's something we need to discuss. May I sit down?"

She saw the bewilderment in his eyes. "Of course." He gestured to the leather fireside chairs. Claire sat in one, smoothing down the skirt of her gray wool dress, steeling herself to say what must be said.

He sat in the other chair, crossed his legs, waited as he watched her thoughtfully.

She wet her lips. Willed herself to keep her voice

even. "I'd like to be released from our agreement, Nick."

He stiffened. Shock flashed through his eyes. "What do you mean?"

Be strong. "I want a divorce."

His facial muscles tightened. "Why?" Then suddenly, he relaxed, and sympathy and compassion were mirrored in the blue depths of his eyes. "Claire, I know you've been devastated by your mother's death. But give yourself time. Things will get better. I promise you."

"That's what you said at the hospital, and you were wrong then."

He flinched, and she knew she'd hurt him. But she'd had to do it. She had to make this a clean break. Better to hurt him than keep him tied through pity to a woman who couldn't fulfill his heart's desire.

"The death of my mother has made me see things clearly," she said. Twisting the knife deeper, she made her voice as cold and impersonal as she could. "Our marriage is a sham. We don't love each other, and I'm not free to make a real marriage as long as I'm tied to you." *I'm sorry, Nick. I'm so sorry. But you'll get over this quickly. It's not as if you love me. This will hurt your pride, but you'll recover.* "My mother's dead, and I haven't gotten pregnant." She smiled cynically. "Yes, my period started yesterday. So you see, there's no longer any reason for us to stay married. Our marriage is a travesty."

His eyes looked like blue ice. "So, you're saying that since you no longer need me to pay your mother's bills, you want out?"

"Yes." She met his gaze without cringing. *I was*

right. He doesn't love me at all. Otherwise he would have said something . . . anything.

"I see." His lips twisted. His face closed. She could see the mask slip into place.

She hadn't realized this would hurt so much. She wanted to cry, *You're wrong. You're wrong. I love you. I'm doing this for you.* But she didn't. This was too important. She owed Nick. She knew how honorable he was. She knew he would never desert her, never go back on their deal. It didn't matter what their prenuptial agreement said. She knew as well as she knew her own name that he wouldn't leave her no matter how much he wanted a child of his own.

So, she had to go through with this. She had to insult him, wound his pride, give him a tangible reason to feel well rid of her once he got over the shock to his ego. And she would have to learn to live with the knowledge that he despised her. She would also have to learn to live without him. The only man she would ever love.

Claire wouldn't let Lucille help her pack. She took some of the clothes Nick had bought her, but left most. She certainly wouldn't need all the cocktail dresses and formal gowns. Nor would she need the furs and jewelry. And even if she did, she wasn't entitled to them. Bad enough that she would have to try to figure out how to repay him for all of Kitty's expenses over the past six months.

When she was finished packing, she called her aunt.

"I don't understand, Claire. Why are you leaving? What's happened?" her aunt Susan said.

"I'll tell you when I get there. Are you sure it's okay for me to come and stay there for a while?"

"Darling, of course, it's okay. You can stay here as long as you like. Permanently, if you want to."

Claire closed her eyes. She wasn't completely alone as long as she had Susan and Dale. And Peachey. How could she forget Peachey?

After phoning her aunt, she wrote Nick a note and left it propped on his side of the bed. It said:

> Nick,
> *I know I'm not entitled to keep the car, but I'll need to use it for a while. As soon as I get another, I'll return the Mercedes.*
>
> Then, as an afterthought, she added:
> *Thank you for everything. I'm sorry it's worked out this way.*
>
> *Claire*

She didn't cry. Not even when Lucille and Mrs. Swift, both with tears in their eyes, hugged her. Not even when she removed her engagement ring and put it in her jewelry box for Nick to find. Not even when she removed the keys to the house from her key ring and placed them in the center of her dresser. Not even when she passed the closed door of Nick's study.

She burrowed deep into her down parka as she loaded her suitcases into the Mercedes. Then she took one last took at the house. She raised her eyes to the tower room, then lowered them to Nick's study on the bottom level. The windows looked blankly back at her.

She wondered if he were standing inside his study. Was he watching her leave? What was he thinking? Her heart beat with heavy thuds, and tears burned behind her eyelids, but she couldn't let herself give way to them.

She knew if ever she allowed herself to cry, she might never be able to stop.

Nick watched her leave. A bone-chilling coldness had settled into his stomach and chest, closing around his heart. He watched the car as it slowly drove away, saw the winking amber of her left turn signal, then the quick flashes of green through the hedges that ringed the yard.

He stared out the window for a long time. The house was silent around him. After awhile, he climbed the stairs into the top of the tower.

Claire's room. Since their marriage, the room and Claire had become permanently intertwined in his mind. He walked softly around, touching the loveseat where they'd shared so many intimate talks, the desk where Claire sat to write in her journal or to answer correspondence, the silver coffee service she'd handled so many times.

A faint scent of roses hung in the air. Her scent. Suddenly, he couldn't stay there another minute. Blindly, he charged down the steep staircase, oblivious to the danger of his recklessness. He climbed the main staircase and walked into their private wing.

When he entered their bedroom, he stopped. Traces of her were everywhere. Then he saw the note. Slowly, he walked toward the bed. He read the note twice, then crushed it in his fist. Anger and pain, hot and heavy, surged through him. And when his eyes rested on the music box he'd given Claire for Christmas, he knew he couldn't stay there.

Grabbing a leather jacket from his closet, he tore back down the steps. He called a message to Mrs. Swift on his way out the back door. "I'm going out. Don't fix dinner for me."

Climbing in the Maserati, he strapped himself in and started the powerful engine. Within thirty minutes he was on the open highway driving west. Where he was headed, he didn't know. He only knew he had to get as far away from Houston as he could.

Claire found a job within two weeks. Finding the job was easy. Surviving the two weeks wasn't.

Her first hurdle was facing her aunt and uncle. Haltingly, she explained the situation. She told them everything, including the terms of her agreement with Nick.

"Claire!" Susan gasped. "I can't believe this. Why, I would have sworn the two of you were deeply in love."

"Yes. I agree," her uncle said quietly, his gray eyes thoughtful as they rested on Claire's face.

Claire looked away as pain constricted her heart. "No," she said quietly. "It was all a pretense. A contract."

She could tell they still didn't believe her, but thank goodness they didn't argue with her. But she caught them watching her when they thought she wasn't looking, and she knew they both had doubts about what she was doing.

Her second hurdle was Peachey.

"Claire Kendrick Callahan, I'd like to turn you over my knee and spank you!" Peachey declared, dark eyes flashing. "What in the world are you thinkin' of, girl?"

"I had to leave, Peachey. I had to! Don't you understand?"

"I understand that you're crazy. Can you look me in the eye and say you aren't in love with your husband?"

Claire couldn't, but she tried anyway.

"You'll have to do better than that, sugar, if you expect this old friend to believe you."

Claire broke down then, and Peachey put her arms around her, and pretty soon they were both crying.

"This is ridiculous, you know that?" Peachey said when the tears were finally dried up and the two were once more talking quietly. "You love him. And he certainly gave you no reason to think he wanted out. And you'd only been married six months. Hardly long enough to give up on this pregnancy business. Weren't you just a tad hasty, Claire?"

Claire shrugged. "I don't know. All I know is how I feel, Peachey. Nick doesn't love me. I gave him every chance to say he did. Every chance to ask me to stay. And he didn't. He agreed with me."

"Do you blame him? You practically told him he was no longer useful to you. The man has pride, sugar. What did you expect him to do? Cry and beg you to stay? That isn't his style. The Nick Callahans of this world never beg."

"No, Peachey. I know I'm right. He doesn't love me, and I can't bear to live there any longer. I don't want to talk about it anymore. I did what I had to do, and it's over. The marriage really never had a chance."

"Has he filed for a divorce yet?"

"I don't know."

Peachey gave her a speculative look. "If he had, you'd know, because they'd send the papers. Maybe he's not going to."

A small spark of hope flared in Claire's breast. But it was quickly extinguished. "He will."

"How can you be so sure?"

"Because last week he sent over all the clothes and furs and jewelry I'd left at the house. Everything. He also sent a note saying he wouldn't take the car back.'' Her heart thumped heavily as she remembered the icy tone of the note. ''He said all of it, including the Mercedes, belonged to me 'for services rendered.' '' She swallowed against the lump in her throat. How could she resent his cruel barb? She'd hurt his pride, insulted him, and he was obviously lashing back at her.

''Whoa,'' Peachey said. ''The dude is decidedly hacked off. So what are you gonna do? Keep the loot? Or send it back?''

''I'd like to send it back. But I know what'll happen if I do. He'll just dump it all on my doorstep again.'' She slumped down in her chair and rubbed her temples. Weariness stole over her. ''I haven't got the energy to fight him. I think I'll just donate it all to Buffalo Children's Home.''

The hardest thing Claire had to do was go to Pinehaven and talk with Dr. Phillips. Walking into the nursing home brought so many memories back, and tears stung her eyes. Kitty's face, green eyes glowing, as she touched Claire's wedding veil. The kindness and patience of Nick as he and Claire visited her mother together so many times. The last time she'd seen Kitty here . . . She shook off the thoughts. She had the future to face. Obligations to meet. There was no time for regrets.

''I need to know exactly how much money my husband paid you over the past six or seven months,'' Claire said to Dr. Phillips.

Then she called the hospital, and after getting the runaround and talking to five different people, she finally got a nice man named Richard Edwards who said he'd send her a copy of her mother's hospital bill. ''Even though it's already paid in full,'' he emphasized.

TWELVE

"Are you sure this is what you want, Nick?"

Nick evaded Tim's eyes. Instead, he steepled his hands and stared out the windows. The skyline was barely visible through gray clouds. It had been raining for days. He remembered that it was a day much like this one when he'd first called Claire into his office and asked her to write the fake article about him. A year ago. It was hard to believe he'd only known Claire one year.

"Have you talked to Claire since she left?" Tim persisted.

Nick finally looked at Tim. A frown marred his smooth, freckled face. "No."

"Why not?"

"What's there to talk about? She made herself perfectly clear. She wants nothing more to do with me."

Tim's frown deepened. "There's something about all this that bothers me. Something that doesn't seem quite right."

189

"Such as?" Nick didn't really care what Tim thought—what anyone thought. Claire was gone. Their marriage was over.

Tim leaned back in his chair and bit his lip. He sighed. "You know I wasn't in favor of this marriage," he began. "I didn't trust Claire at all, or your assessment of her."

Nick nodded. His assessment had obviously been wrong. He had a sudden clear picture of Claire on their wedding day. Her purity. Her luminous smile. Had it all been an act? Could he have been so blind? Pain knotted in his chest.

Tim was still talking. "But once I got to know her, I changed my mind. And I don't change my mind easily. You know that, too."

Nick nodded again. Yes, they'd both been taken in. It was ironic really. Nick Callahan—the shrewd businessman—had been bested at his own game. While he'd been congratulating himself on his clever handling of his malleable wife, she had even more cleverly manipulated him. She had given him exactly what she'd known he wanted—the belief that he had the upper hand. She'd used him, and when she no longer needed him, she'd discarded him.

"The point is, Claire is a fine person. Too fine to dump you simply because she doesn't need you anymore. I think her emotions are a mess. I think her mother's death has done a number on her mind and she's not thinking straight. I think you should try to talk to her."

He wanted to believe Tim was right. But Tim hadn't seen her face when she called their marriage a travesty. No. She didn't love him. She wanted to be free. "I'm not going to beg."

Tim stared at him for a long moment. "There's a difference between fighting for something you believe in and begging. I thought you knew that."

"Why fight to save something that never existed?"

"I saw the way she looked at you, Nick. The way you looked at her. The two of you had more going than a simple marriage of convenience. And if your pride wasn't hurt so badly, you'd admit it." Tim gave him a cunning look. "I never thought you were a quitter. I can't believe you're giving her up without a fight. Believe me, if Claire was my wife, I wouldn't give up unless she married someone else." Tim laughed, the sound self-deprecating. "And maybe not even then."

"Well, I'm not you."

Tim stood. His voice hardened. "How well I know that." He picked up the papers he'd brought into the office. "So you want me to draw up the divorce documents?"

"Yes." Why didn't Tim just leave him alone?

"Nick, I've given this a lot of thought, and I decided that if you were determined on this course of action, you'd have to get yourself another lawyer."

Nick's jaw tightened. "*You're* my lawyer."

Tim took a deep breath. His dark eyes glittered as they met Nick's squarely. "In all fairness to you, I can't represent you on this. There would be a conflict of interest."

"Explain yourself."

"I'm interested in Claire, even if you aren't. If it's really over between the two of you, I'd like to see her." Tim's chin lifted. "You don't mind, do you?"

"Why should I mind? She's nothing to me. She never was." He pretended an interest in the report he'd been reading before Tim came into his office. "If you don't want to handle the divorce, fine. I'll ask Angelo to take care of it.''

After Tim left, Nick abandoned the report. He walked over to the window and stared unseeingly at the bleak day.

Bleak. Gray. Cold.

He rubbed his temples. Bitterness welled into his throat. Once again his personal life was a dismal failure. What the hell was wrong with him that he continued to set himself up for a fall? He'd always prided himself on his good sense, his ability to see a situation, assess it, and make good decisions. And once more, he'd walked headlong into disaster.

Well, he had finally learned his lesson. Never again.

The words mocked him. Too late, they said. The damage has already been done. You did it again. You allowed your emotions to become involved. And, bingo, you lost your edge.

How had it happened? When had it happened? He had thought he was so smart. He had picked a woman with his brains, offered her money and security, and then he had married her. He had scoffed at her questions about love when he'd first proposed, told her he'd give her something better.

He was a fool. He had married a woman who believed in love, but by forcing her to give him only what he thought he wanted, he had killed any chance he'd had that she could love him. The laugh was definitely on him.

He had fallen in love with his wife but too late. Now he had to pay the price. Now he would have to stand by and watch her fall in love with someone else.

Punching his right fist into the palm of his left hand,

Nick fought the tightness in his chest and the hot tide of misery that threatened to engulf him.

Then he turned away from the window, grabbed his briefcase, and charged out of the office, down the short hallway to the reception area.

Wanda looked up, obviously startled, hands poised over her keyboard. Her dark eyebrows arched up.

"I'm leaving for the day," Nick said. Before she could answer, he stalked off.

For the first month after she left Nick, Claire avoided the Buffalo Children's Home. Then one day she realized she was depriving herself unnecessarily. Nick never visited the home except on the weekends. He worked too late most weekdays. So she was perfectly safe stopping there on her way home from work.

The following Tuesday she did just that and spent an hour and a half visiting with the children she'd come to love so much. They all wanted to know where she'd been.

"I started a new job, so I've been very busy," she explained, keeping her voice light.

"I missed you a lot," Brigette said. "I even called the house one day, but whoever answered the phone said you weren't there."

A dull pain throbbed in Claire's breast. "Honey, I'm sorry. It was thoughtless of me not to come sooner."

Brigette, who was too sharp to be fooled easily, said, "Nick hasn't been around much lately, either."

At the mention of Nick's name, Claire's heart bumped painfully against her chest wall. She was on the verge of fabricating another excuse but something in Brigette's eyes stopped her. Claire couldn't lie to her. Brigette deserved the truth. "Nick and I are sepa-

rated, Brigette. And . . . well . . . things have been
. . . difficult.''

Brigette's blue eyes widened, and an expression of
dismay distorted her pretty face. ''Oh, no! Why?''

Claire sighed. ''We made a mistake, that's all.''

''A mistake! But, Claire—''

''Sometimes adults do stupid things, honey. Then
they have to try to correct the problems they created.''

''I . . . I can't believe it . . .'' Without warning,
Brigette's eyes filled with tears.

Claire's throat constricted at the obvious pain the
teenager was feeling. Impulsively, she drew the slender
girl into her arms. Her own eyes filled. ''I'm sorry,''
she whispered. ''I'm sorry we let you down.'' Now the
destruction of the child's illusions was one more thing
Claire had to feel guilty about.

''I . . . I thought . . .'' Brigette pulled away, and
their eyes met. The girl swallowed. A tear rolled down
her cheek.

''What, honey?'' Claire gently wiped the tear away.

Brigette's bottom lip trembled. She turned away,
blinking furiously. ''Oh, nothing. It . . . it's stupid.
I'm stupid.''

Claire touched her arm, and Brigette bowed her head.
Now the tears came freely. Claire put her arms around
the girl and hugged her. She couldn't hold back her
own tears. ''It's okay,'' she soothed, rubbing Brigette's
back. ''But I wish you'd tell me what you're thinking.''

''Oh, it's so dumb,'' was the muffled reply. ''I . . .
I thought . . . I used to dream about you and Nick. I
. . . oh, I know you would never have been my parents,
but . . .'' Her voice trailed off, and Claire tightened her
arms. Dear God. How cruel they'd been. Unknowingly,
perhaps, but still cruel.

Before she left the home that day, she asked the receptionist if she could talk with Mr. or Mrs. Civic. Ten minutes later, Gerri Civic, an attractive fortyish woman with a sweet smile, walked into the reception area.

"Hello, Mrs. Callahan. This is a nice surprise. We've missed seeing you! The children have asked about you many times."

Keep piling on the guilt, Claire thought.

"What can I do for you?"

"Can we go into your office?" Claire suggested.

"Certainly."

When the two were settled into Gerri Civic's small office, Claire said, "Mrs. Civic, would it be possible for Brigette to have a weekend pass? I'd like to have her come and spend the weekend with me."

"Well . . . it's unusual to grant a pass for a visit to anyone other than family, but in your case . . . I don't see why not." Gerri Civic smiled. "After all, you and Mr. Callahan are our greatest benefactors."

I should tell her Nick and I are no longer living together. It's not fair to let her think . . . "Thank you. I appreciate it. Would it be all right if I pick her up about five-thirty on Friday?" Claire stood, extending her hand.

"Perfectly all right." The director stood, too, and the two women shook hands.

"Where's Brigette?" Nick asked Lisa after the first exuberant greetings were over. He shouldn't have stayed away so long.

Lisa's expressive dark eyes widened. "She's at your house!"

"My house!"

"Yeah. Claire came and got her last night. She's

spending the weekend with you. Did you forget?'' Lisa grinned impishly.

Nick's head whirled. Claire came and picked up Brigette? For the weekend? What was going on? "I haven't talked to Claire," he improvised.

He wanted to leave right then. Was something wrong? But he didn't want to alarm the children, so he visited with them for a couple of hours. When the visit was over he headed straight for Paul Civic's office.

"Nick! Good to see you!" Civic said, standing immediately when Nick entered his office. "We haven't seen much of you lately."

"Why did Claire take Brigette for the weekend?" Nick said without preamble. "Who gave her permission?"

Civic's face paled. "Why . . . uh, Gerri did. Is . . . is something wrong?" He frowned. "Your . . . your wife picked her up. I saw her myself. I thought you—"

"You thought wrong. My wife and I are separated. We're in the middle of divorce proceedings."

"But surely there's no harm in Brigette spending the weekend with Mrs . . . uh . . . Callahan . . ."

"Let's hope not," Nick said. He knew he was acting irrationally, but he couldn't seem to help himself. Were Claire and what he had lost going to haunt him forever? Would he run into her and memories of their marriage at every turn? Worse, would she unknowingly build Brigette's hopes, the way she'd built his, then let her down?

He had to put a stop to this. Now.

Claire's aunt and uncle had gone to visit old friends in New Braunfels for the weekend, leaving the house to Claire and Brigette. Saturday was such a beautiful day—sunny and mild for early February—that she and Brigette had decided to spend most of it outdoors. After cooking breakfast, they put on jeans and sneakers and sweatshirts, and Claire drove to the zoo, where they spent hours walking and talking and looking at the animals.

Claire enjoyed the fresh air and the change of scenery. For the first time in weeks, she felt almost happy. Maybe there *could* be a life without Nick, she thought. Of course, she wouldn't always have the comfort of the bright teenager's company. She quickly dismissed the depressing thought. Take one day at a time. Remember your philosophy.

"Do you miss your mother, Claire?" Brigette asked as they walked along.

"Very much." It didn't hurt quite so much to talk about Kitty as it had when she had first died.

"I miss my mother, too." Brigette shoved her hands in the back pockets of her jeans and watched two grizzly bears roll around on the sun-warmed rocks. She smiled, and Claire looked at her perfect profile. The child was so beautiful. Beautiful enough and graceful enough to be a model. Maybe Claire should mention Brigette to Peachey.

"Do you want to tell me about your mother?" Claire asked.

Brigette turned toward her. She nodded.

"Let's go get something to drink and find a place to sit down," Claire suggested.

Over Diet Cokes they talked.

"My mother died when I was eight. But I still remember her. She was really nice. We didn't have much money. She . . . she used to draw paper dolls for me." Brigette grinned. "The other kids in the neighborhood were jealous.

"After she died, things changed. I guess my dad tried, but he didn't know how to take care of me and my brother. He started drinking a lot." Sadness flitted across Brigette's face.

"What happened?"

"When I was ten and my brother Sean was fifteen, my dad was killed in a barroom fight." She said it with no emotion, and Claire's heart twisted. "Sean and me didn't have any money, and we didn't have anyone to help us."

"No family?" A lock of hair fell across Brigette's forehead, and Claire wanted to brush it back, wanted to caress the girl's cheek, wanted to tell her everything would be okay.

"No. My mother had a sister—our aunt Kathleen—but she went off to California or some place, and we didn't have any idea how to get in touch with her." Brigette looked at Claire, her blue eyes clear. "Dad always said Aunt Kathleen was a hooker."

Shock barreled through Claire. Not that Brigette might have an aunt who was a prostitute, but that the child was so matter-of-fact about it. She'd said *hooker* like she might have said *teacher*.

"Anyway, Sean started dealing coke to make money, but then I guess he got hooked on it, and before long the neighbors called the child welfare people, and they came and Sean was sent to a rehab center, and I came to live at the home."

"And you've been there ever since?"

Brigette nodded glumly. "I guess Sean's out now, 'cause he's eighteen. I kept thinkin' maybe he'd come and get me, or maybe someone nice would adopt me." Once more her clear, blue eyes met Claire's. "Then, when I met you, after you and Nick got married, I started to dream about what it would be like to have somebody like the two of you for a mother and father.''

Claire reached across the iron table and clasped Brigette's hands in hers. She wished she could think of something to say. But everything had already been said.

Claire felt tired. A good feeling, she decided. Instead of the weariness that had permeated her bones for weeks, she felt honest-to-goodness physically tired.

She looked at Brigette sitting in the passenger seat of the Mercedes. She smiled. The teenager was so lovable. It hurt Claire to know how many children had been abandoned, either emotionally or physically. If only she could do something about this one. Claire knew it was impossible for one person to solve all the problems in the world, but if each person solved just one . . . She reached across and squeezed Brigette's hand.

"What do you want to do tonight, honey? Go out to eat? Get a pizza and rent a couple of movies?'' Claire's aunt and uncle had a VCR, and Claire had been indulging herself for weeks.

"I . . . I'd love to go out to eat,'' Brigette confessed shyly.

She probably didn't get to eat out often, Claire thought. Why didn't I think to take her or the other kids out before? "All right. Why don't you pick the place?'' She turned onto the street where her aunt and uncle lived.

But Brigette was no longer listening. "Claire, look . . .'' She pointed out the front window.

Puzzled, Claire looked down the street. A silver Lotus was parked in front of her aunt's house. Claire's heart leaped up into her throat. Leaning against the

Lotus was a tall, dark-haired man who she'd recognize anywhere.

What was he doing here?

"It's Nick," Brigette said, voice lilting.

Claire pulled in the driveway and cut the engine. Brigette wrenched open her door and went flying toward Nick. "Hi, gorgeous," he said, hugging her close. His compelling eyes met Claire's over the top of Brigette's head.

"Hello, Nick," Claire said quietly, although her pulse was racing and her insides were quaking. He was wearing soft, well-worn jeans, polished brown loafers, and a cream-colored sweater under a tan corduroy jacket. His hair glistened in the late afternoon sunlight.

"Hello, Claire."

She stood awkwardly. She wasn't sure what he wanted, and she didn't know what to say.

Finally he spoke. "I went by the home today. They told me Brigette was with you."

"Oh." Oh, dear. She could see by the way his eyes had darkened that he wasn't pleased.

"Brigette," he said, "do you mind going on into the house. I'd like to talk to Claire privately."

Brigette looked at him, then at Claire. Claire gave her an encouraging smile. "It's okay, honey. I'll be in in a minute."

Brigette frowned, but she complied. When the front door closed behind her, Nick turned toward Claire once more. "What kind of game are you playing here?"

Claire stiffened. "What do you mean? I'm not playing a game."

"You must be. You never brought Brigette home with you while you were living with me. So the only conclusion I can draw is that you're using her."

"Using her!" Claire's nervousness disappeared. "What have I ever done to cause you to believe I'd use a child—for any reason?"

"You used me, didn't you?"

Claire stared at him. She knew she'd wounded his pride. She knew he was angry. She also knew she couldn't let Brigette be hurt. "I was only thinking of Brigette when I asked her out," she said quietly. "When I visited the home on Tuesday, Brigette and I talked, and when she asked me, I told her the truth—that you and I are separated and in the process of getting a divorce. She cried when she found out."

Claire looked away, the memory of Brigette's pain knifing through her once more, mingling with her own pain. "When I asked her why she was so upset, she . . ." Claire slowly met Nick's gaze once more. ". . . She said she had dreamed of becoming our daughter."

The color drained from Nick's face.

Claire was relentless. Let him hurt, too. She no longer remembered that she'd left him to keep from hurting him. She no longer remembered that she wanted him to think of her as being selfish. She no longer remembered that she didn't need to look good in his eyes. All she knew was that she was hurting, Brigette was hurting, and he would have to take his share of the blame for all the problems they'd caused.

After all, it was *his* idea that they make a marriage of convenience. Not hers.

"So your solution to the kid's daydream is to dangle a carrot under her nose? Make it even harder for her to accept that her dream isn't going to come true?"

His words were cutting and icy cold.

"You can really be a bastard, can't you?"

"I never pretended to be anything but," he snapped.

"Unlike you, who pretended to be all sorts of things you weren't."

All Claire's joy in the day faded. She could feel her shoulders slumping under the weight of Nick's dislike and disapproval. What could she say? There was so much subterfuge and distrust between them, nothing she said would even make a dent. "Brigette's lonely, Nick. You and I let her down. I was only trying to make it up to her a little bit. That's all. No sinister motive."

"You don't have to worry about Brigette any longer. You're right about one thing. I *did* let her down. So I'll take care of her from now on." He began to walk toward the house.

"Where are you going?" Claire said, alarm coursing through her.

"To get Brigette. I'm taking her home."

"No, you're not!"

He jerked to a halt, turned slowly. His eyes glittered.

"If you go into that house, if you try to take Brigette away, I'll call the police."

"You wouldn't dare."

"Try me."

For several long seconds, they stared at each other. Claire could see a muscle twitching under his left eye. He was very angry. But Claire was very angry, too. And she would not allow Brigette to be caught in the middle of the mess they'd made of their lives.

Finally he moved toward the car, and Claire could feel relief washing over her, and weakness coming in its wake.

"We're not finished," he said in a parting shot before opening the door to the Lotus. "But the next round will be in court."

THIRTEEN

Claire's anger faded quickly. How could she stay angry with Nick? He was only acting in character. Besides, she was the one who had made him suspicious of her motives. She couldn't have it both ways. If she wanted him to believe she felt nothing where he was concerned, why shouldn't he think she was the same way where Brigette was concerned?

For the rest of the weekend, Claire couldn't get the memory of Nick's coldness and indifference out of her mind. She had obviously done her job well, for it was apparent to her that he was completely over her.

Of course, he never loved you anyway. So it's not surprising it didn't take long for him to decide to cut his losses, chalk you up as a mistake and move on with his life.

If only she could move on with hers.

If only she didn't still love him.

Two days later Claire was served with divorce papers. Her heart thudded as she stared at them. Each beat was like a blow to her heart. It was really happening. She hadn't realized the divorce would hurt so much.

Isn't this what you wanted?

She only gave the papers a cursory glance, making note of the fact that she was due at a preliminary meeting the following Monday morning. Then she set the papers down. She couldn't bear to look at them any longer.

"Do you mind if I take a look at those, Claire?" her Uncle Dale asked.

"No." *Oh, Nick. If only things could have been different. If only I'd been able to give you a child.*

After her uncle read through the papers, he said, "Who's representing you in this divorce?"

Claire shrugged. "I don't have a lawyer."

"You'd better get one. This all looks fairly complicated to me. Do you want me to find an attorney for you?"

"No. I don't want anything from Nick anyway, so why do I need a lawyer?" *I just want to forget. As quickly as possible.*

"Claire, you're not thinking straight, honey. Of course you must have someone to represent your interests."

"I told you, Uncle Dale. I don't want a cent from Nick. I'm not entitled to anything of his. A lawyer would be a waste of money." Nick's face, with its grooves and hollows, haunted her. She'd thought she was doing so well, forgetting him, but seeing him the other day had proven her wrong.

The very next day she received a call from Tim Sutherland. "Your aunt gave me your number at work," he said. "Do you mind?"

"No. But could you hold on a minute?" She got up and shut the door to her office, then picked up the phone again. "How have you been, Tim?" She felt absurdly pleased that he'd called her. He was a link to Nick.

"I've been fine, Claire, but I didn't call to talk about me. I'm concerned about you. Who's your lawyer?"

"For the divorce, you mean?"

"Yes."

"I don't have one, Tim. I really don't need one."

"Of course you need one."

"No, really, I don't."

"Listen, Claire, that's the dumbest thing I've ever heard you say. You can't go to that meeting without a lawyer. They'll chew you up and spit you out before you even know what's happening."

"I won't have a lawyer," she said stubbornly.

"Will you at least let me go to the meeting with you?"

"You! But . . . I thought—"

"No, I'm not representing Nick." A hardness settled into Tim's voice. "I told him my sympathies lay with you, so it wouldn't be ethical to represent him."

"Oh, Tim . . ." How Tim's statements must have hurt Nick. His best friend! Nick would view this as a betrayal, Claire knew it. "Listen, it's so sweet of you, but I can't—"

"You can. I won't take no for an answer. I can't represent you—I drew up the prenuptial agreement, so representing you would be a conflict of interest—but I can advise you. And if it turns out you need an attorney, I can recommend one to you."

And no matter what Claire said, Tim insisted he would be at the meeting. Claire thought about it, and she realized it would be a good idea for Tim to be there. She intended to get some things straight with Nick, and she wanted the arrangements to be legally endorsed. She would need Tim's help.

Claire's new boss wasn't thrilled about her asking for the following Monday morning off, but he didn't refuse. For the rest of the week, Claire could think of little else but the meeting and the fact that she'd see Nick again. She and Tim talked several times that week, and on Thursday after work he came over to her aunt's house.

When she opened the door and saw him, she realized how much she'd missed him. They hugged, and Claire wished with all her heart that everything had worked out differently.

Later Tim took her out for dinner. He took pains to entertain her, and she was grateful for his friendship. But even though she enjoyed the evening, it was with a bittersweet pleasure, for she knew she could never see Tim without thinking of Nick. Without being reminded of what she'd lost.

Tim briefed her on what to expect at the meeting. "Remember, Claire, don't agree to anything without getting my okay."

They made arrangements to meet Monday morning at nine forty-five in the lobby of the building where the law offices were housed.

Claire was early and nervous. When Tim arrived, he squeezed her arm and smiled down at her, his brown eyes warm and comforting. "Don't worry," he said. "It'll be okay."

The law offices of Angelo, Ford, and Angelo were dignified and elegant, just what Claire had expected. She and Tim were ushered into a sunny corner office where a big, dark-haired man was sitting with Nick at a rectangular conference table.

After the introductions were made, Claire and Tim sat across from Nick and Bill Angelo, his attorney. Claire's gaze met Nick's, and for just a second, she saw a flash of pain in the depths of his eyes, but it was quickly banished. A dull ache throbbed in her chest. What a mess they'd made of their lives.

Bill Angelo cleared his throat, looked at Nick, then began speaking. Claire watched his face. She couldn't look at Nick. If she were to keep her equilibrium and not make a fool of herself today, she'd better avoid those eyes she'd never been able to resist.

"Since there is an airtight prenuptial agreement between the two of you, Mrs. Callahan," Bill Angelo said, "this meeting is simply routine." He began enumerating the terms of the agreement, all of which Claire knew by heart. When he finished, he put the papers down. "Based on this, my client is prepared to make a complete settlement today." He turned toward Nick.

Claire twisted her hands in her lap. She glanced at Tim. He knew what she wanted him to do, and he'd argued with her about it, but he'd finally agreed.

Nick opened his briefcase. He drew out something that looked like a check and handed it across to Tim. Tim looked at it briefly, then handed it to her, his face impassive.

Claire accepted the check. It was a cashier's check made out to her for the sum of $250,000.00 At the bottom was typed: FINAL SETTLEMENT—CALLAHAN VS. CALLAHAN. FOR SERVICES RENDERED. For a moment, Claire couldn't move. The blood rushed through her veins, and a great wave of dizziness rocked her. She closed her eyes and took a deep breath.

She had to remember that Nick was striking back. She had wounded his pride deeply, and he was getting even the only way he knew how.

Shakily, she stood. Her eyes met Nick's.

Slowly, deliberately, she tore the check into four pieces, letting the pieces float to the table. Fighting tears, Claire said, "I don't want your money. I don't want anything from you, Nick. In fact, as Tim will tell you, I plan to pay back every cent you spent on me or my mother if it takes me the rest of my life. All I want is my freedom."

Then she picked up her purse and walked out of the office.

For the next two days, Claire walked around like a zombie. She couldn't eat, she couldn't sleep, she couldn't concentrate on her work. By Wednesday night she knew she had to do something to snap out of her misery. She couldn't go on like this. Her marriage was over, but not her life. She was acting as if the world had come to an end, and it was time to stop.

She decided to visit Buffalo Children's Home. Just thinking about seeing Brigette and the other children cheered her up. Maybe she could take Brigette out for dinner.

But when Claire got there, she was told she couldn't take Brigette out.

Paul Civic gave her the news. "I'm sorry, Mrs. Callahan—"

"Ms. Kendrick," Claire corrected. "Is there some sort of problem?"

"Uh . . . no . . . Ms. Kendrick . . . uh . . . I'm really sorry, but I can't give you permission to take

any of the children out. Today . . . or any other day."
He didn't meet her eyes.

"Why not?"

He looked at her and shrugged. "It's a judgment call,
that's all. As you know, passes are strictly optional, and
we've decided it's not in our best interest to allow you
to take Brigette off the grounds. I'm sorry."

Nick. This had to be Nick's doing. He hated her.

She didn't tell Brigette about the conversation.
Above all, she did not want Brigette to have to choose
up sides. Nick's action had accomplished one good
thing, though. When she left the home that evening,
Claire was determined to get her life straightened out.
For her own survival, she would make herself forget
Nick Callahan and their short-lived, ill-fated
marriage.

On Friday of that week, Tim called her at work. "I
have tickets for *Grand Hotel* Saturday night at Jones
Hall. Would you like to go with me?"

The musical had won five Tony awards and Claire
had never seen it. She should be excited about the prospect of the evening, but it was hard to be enthusiastic
about anything. She accepted the invitation, though.

Her aunt was delighted when Claire told her about
her plans. "I'm glad. You need to get out more,"
Susan said. "It's not healthy to sit home and brood."

"I'm not divorced yet, you know. Technically, I
shouldn't be going out with other men."

"You're just going out with a friend," her aunt
countered. "There's nothing wrong in that." She gave
Claire a shrewd look. "This man *is* just a friend, isn't
he?"

"Yes, of course."

So Claire went. She even enjoyed herself, only thinking about Nick once, when during a poignant scene, it was obvious the baron and the ballerina were star-crossed lovers. When the baron died, Claire knew exactly how his lover felt. Nick was dead to her, too, and it hurt. Deeply. She wondered if she'd ever again be able to see a sad movie or read a sad book without feeling this clutching pain, this raw desolation?

Afterwards Tim took her for a late supper at Charley's 517, and Claire was glad it was a restaurant she and Nick had never gone to together. By the time Tim took her home, it was very late, and Claire was tired. Maybe she'd even sleep that night, she thought.

Tim walked her to the door, and they stood outside for a few moments, talking. The light from the street lamp cast shadows over his earnest face, and Claire realized it was good to have a friend like Tim. But she wondered how their friendship would affect his friendship with Nick. She didn't want to cause any problems between them.

Finally, she said, "Well, I'd better be going in. Thanks for a lovely evening, Tim. It was nice of you to take pity on me."

"I asked you because I'd rather be with you than anyone I can think of," Tim said. "Not because I was sorry for you."

Oh, dear, Claire thought. *I hope he doesn't mean what I think he means.*

Tim bent to kiss her, and Claire stiffened, even as she told herself to tread lightly. Tim was so nice; she didn't want to hurt him any more than was necessary. His lips touched hers briefly, softly, and Claire felt sad because she knew she would never feel passion for this man. She gently pulled back.

"Claire—" His voice sounded rough.

"I'd better go in," she said, touching his cheek. "Thanks again, Tim."

"Wait. Please, Claire . . ." He reached for her hands. "I . . . I had a wonderful time tonight."

I can't deal with this.

"I hope we can do this often." He squeezed her hands, then released them, and she shoved them in her pockets. "How about this coming Friday?"

"Tim," Claire said firmly, "I can't."

"Well, that's okay. If you're busy Friday, what about Saturday, or even Sunday?" His voice was eager.

"Tim. Listen to me. You must listen to me."

He sighed.

"I don't want to lead you on, Tim. I value you as a friend, but I don't think it's a good idea for us to see too much of one another."

He was silent for a long time. Then, with resignation, he said, "It's Nick, isn't it?"

She owed Tim honesty. "Yes," she said quietly. "It's Nick." Her heart constricted in her chest as she said the words. "It will always be Nick. I'm sorry."

"You love him."

"Yes."

"Then why are you going through with this divorce? He told me it was your idea."

Claire took a deep breath. "Tim, I felt I had to tell you the truth about my feelings because I like you and respect you. But my reasons for leaving Nick are my own, and they're personal. I can't share them with you."

She could hear the weariness in his voice as he said, "Fair enough." He laughed, the sound hollow and self-deprecating. "I appreciate the fact that you didn't lie to me."

Claire smiled and reaching up on tiptoe, she kissed his cheek. "I'll never lie to you."

"Nick's a fool."

"Our problems are not his fault, Tim."

"If you say so," he said, but he sounded skeptical. "How about us? Even if we don't date, can we still be friends?"

"Of course."

"And you'll go out with me occasionally?"

"If I can."

But later, as Claire prepared for bed, she knew it probably wasn't going to be possible to continue seeing Tim—under any circumstances—for if she did, he might hold on to the hope that she would change her mind. And she never would.

Nick went skiing for the remainder of the week after the meeting with Claire. But even Sun Valley and perfect skiing conditions didn't take his mind off Claire for more than a couple of hours at a time. Everything seemed to remind him of her. The sunlight dancing across the evergreens reminded him of her eyes and her bright hair. The flickering firelight in the lodge reminded him of their honeymoon suite at the St. Maurice. A young couple, arms around each other, reminded him of those lazy afternoons in Monterey.

When he returned to Houston, he felt rested and less tense, however he was a long way from forgetting about his soon-to-be-ex-wife. But he was determined to wipe Claire out of his mind. All he needed was time, he promised himself as he tackled the stack of correspondence waiting for him on Monday morning.

At ten o'clock he attended the weekly managers'

meeting, and afterwards, Tim approached him and said, "How about lunch?"

"Sure." Relations between them had been strained ever since Tim had told him he didn't want to represent him in the divorce, but Nick was trying to be fair. He and Tim went too far back to let Claire come between them.

Over red beans and rice at Treebeards, Tim said, "I saw Claire Saturday night."

Nick was glad of his ability to keep his expression impassive. All he said was, "Oh?"

"Yes. I took her to see *Grand Hotel*."

Was Tim deliberately baiting him? It wouldn't work. Nick was more experienced in the nuances of playing against an adversary's weaknesses. He knew that in a face-off, he would win out over Tim any day of the week. "Was the show any good?"

Tim laid his fork down. "Christ, Nick, you're a cool one, aren't you? Doesn't it bother you at all that I took your wife out?"

"My estranged wife, soon to be my ex-wife." Nick gave Tim a cynical smile.

Tim's eyes narrowed. "I repeat, doesn't it bother you at all?"

"No. It's a free country."

"I asked her out for Friday night. Maybe I'll even ask her to marry me when your divorce is final. Does *that* bother you?"

Nick froze, and an icy coldness crept through him. "I hope the two of you will be very happy," he said tightly. "I'll be sure and send a wedding present."

"She refused to go out with me again."

She refused to go out with him again. "Why?" His voice sounded odd, and he hoped Tim didn't notice.

"If you don't know why, I can't explain it to you."

For the rest of the day, Nick couldn't forget the look in Tim's eyes when he'd said *if you don't know why, I can't explain it to you*. He thought about the look in Claire's eyes when she tore up his check. He thought about the way she acted when she told him she wanted a divorce. He thought about the kind of person Claire was—the kind of person he'd *thought* she was. He thought about the way she'd cared for her mother. He thought about the pleasure, the happiness, the concern he'd seen in her eyes—over and over again. He thought about everything. Over and over again.

At four o'clock, he pressed the intercom. "Wanda? Would you get Bill Angelo on the line for me?"

The following Friday, Claire rubbed her temples wearily. She'd worked all day on the copy for an advertisement her agency was doing for a local substance abuse hospital, and it still wasn't right. Her concentration was shot.

I've got to get a grip on myself. Other people survive divorce. I will, too.

At four fifty-five she began to clean off her desk, and at five she picked up her briefcase and suit jacket and waved good-bye to her co-workers.

"Got a big weekend planned, Claire?" asked Margie, a pretty brunette artist.

"Not really."

As she rode the elevator down to the parking lot level, Claire thought about how different her life was lately. With her mother gone, she no longer had the nursing home to visit. And with Nick gone, there was no one to demand anything of her. She was perfectly free.

Why was freedom so lonely?

The drive home took her forty-five minutes in the Friday afternoon traffic. Soon she wouldn't have such a long drive. At the end of the month she planned to move into her own apartment. As she drove up the street toward her aunt's house, she was preoccupied and didn't notice the Lotus until she was practically parallel with the house.

Claire's heart slammed into her chest.

He was leaning against the Lotus, watching her approach. With shaking hands, she pulled into the driveway and slowly emerged from the car into the late afternoon sunshine. The air was chilly, but she barely noticed. Her entire being was centered on the man walking toward her. Her mind registered the details of his appearance while her heart pounded with a mixture of fear and a queer kind of happiness.

Her eyes devoured him. He was dressed casually— in khaki pants, white sweater, and a dark leather jacket. As he came closer, Claire saw that his face was somber, his blue eyes riveted on hers.

"Hello, Claire."

"Hello, Nick." *What's he doing here? What does he want now?*

"I had to talk to you."

Claire had recovered some of her aplomb. "Hasn't everything already been said?"

He moved closer—close enough to touch—and now Claire's heart skittered alarmingly. When he reached out and touched her cheek, her entire body reacted as a powerful shudder raced through her. *Oh, God. I can't take this. What kind of game is he playing?* But when she looked into his eyes, she saw no malice, no dislike, no bitterness. Perhaps he saw her confusion, because he smiled.

The smile grabbed her heart and squeezed it.

"Claire, I don't blame you for being suspicious. All I ask is that you hear me out. There are things I have to tell you."

She was afraid. She could so easily lose control, make a total fool of herself.

"Are your aunt and uncle home?"

"Yes."

"Then would you go for a drive with me?"

"Nick—"

"Please, Claire."

Please. Nick Callahan rarely said *please*. Claire swallowed. "I . . . I'd better tell my aunt. She might see the Mercedes and wonder . . ."

"Of course."

A few minutes later, she was back. Mind racing, she allowed him to help her into the Lotus. Before he turned the key in the ignition, he said, "Do you mind if we go to the house? I'm not sure we can talk in the car."

Her brain said *No! Danger!* her heart said, "No. I don't mind."

The twenty-five minute ride seemed interminable. Claire stared out the window. Her thoughts were a jumble. What did he want? What would he say? Why had she come?

She must be crazy.

Finally they reached the house, and Claire's chest hurt just looking at it.

When he led her into the tower, she felt faint. But she offered no resistance when he took her hand and drew her up the twisting spiral staircase.

Everything looked exactly the same. Except for the music box. Claire bit her bottom lip to keep it from trembling. The music box that Nick had given her for Christmas sat in the middle of the low coffee table in front of the loveseat. The last time Claire had seen it, it was sitting on her dresser in their bedroom.

Nick must have moved it.

Why?

She'd have thought he would have put it away, out of sight. Maybe even smashed it.

The semi-precious stones imbedded in the base of the music box winked in the apricot glow of the rays of the setting sun. Slowly, Claire looked from the box to Nick.

"I called Bill Angelo the other day and told him to stop the divorce proceedings," he said.

Shock thundered through her. "Why?"

"I don't want a divorce."

She wet her lips. The blue of his eyes held her spellbound. "Why not?"

He didn't answer.

"Why not?" she repeated.

"Because I love you."

Joy exploded inside her. He loved her. He loved her. Her eyes filled with tears. "Oh, Nick," she said brokenly.

He reached for her hands. "Come sit down," he said gently. "There are a lot of things I have to tell you."

They sat side by side on the loveseat.

Still holding her hands, he began to talk. "I've done nothing but think all week long. And now I think I understand why you asked for a divorce."

When she would have interrupted him, he said, "No. Wait. Let me finish, okay?"

"Okay." She watched his face, his dear face.

"I think I loved you from the very beginning, but was afraid to admit it."

Happiness, pure and simple, flooded her.

He sighed, rubbed his thumbs over the backs of her hands. "There's so much to tell you, but for you to understand, I have to explain about my family. My father was a laborer. He worked on an assembly line, making fans. He drank too much. So did my mother. Their only entertainment was hanging out at the local beer garden four or five nights a week. They used to drag me and my sister along. One night, when he had gone drinking with his buddies after work, he walked in front of a bus. He was killed instantly."

"Oh, Nick, I'm sorry . . ."

He shrugged. "It was a long time ago."

"How old were you?"

"Nine. My mother tried, I guess, but . . . I don't know. It must have all been too much for her. She didn't have any skills. The only work she was qualified to do was cleaning. For a while she worked for a janitorial service. Then one day she just left. When Natalie and I got home from school, she was gone."

Claire thought about Brigette. Thought about how her story and Nick's story were so similar. She wondered if he knew Brigette's background.

"I was eleven. Nat was sixteen. There wasn't much we could do. The social service people put us in foster homes."

"They separated you?" Claire was appalled.

His eyes looked bleak. His hands gripped hers tightly. "Yes. I was miserable. Scared. Lonely. But I toughened up. Fast. In order to survive, I had to. The first home I was in, they were really nice to me. I even got so I liked them. Then something happened. The grandmother of the family had to move in with them, and they couldn't keep me. So I got sent to another, then another."

"Oh, Nick," Claire said again. Her heart bled for the lonely boy he'd been.

"Most of the foster parents were indifferent. The only reason they kept foster kids was for the money."

Claire thought about her own happy, secure childhood. About Kitty. About her father. About how much they'd loved her.

"But I survived. I had one real good thing going for me. I was smart."

Claire smiled.

"Natalie was smart, too. She graduated from high school at seventeen and got a full scholarship to nursing school. She finished the training as well as her degree in three years, so by the time she was twenty, and I was fifteen, she was a nurse. A damn good nurse." Pride tinged his voice, and he finally released Claire's hands. "She had an offer from City Hospital here in Houston, so she got custody of me, and we moved to Houston."

Claire decided she loved Natalie a lot.

"Anyway the rest isn't really that important. She met David, her husband, and they were married. I lived with them summers and holidays. They helped me some financially, although most of my college expenses were paid by scholarships."

He stopped, took her hands again. His touch sent a warming through her body. "The point to this story is that I wanted you to see what had caused me to act the way I did. I'd always wanted a family. A real family of my own. But I was scared, too. I'd made one bad choice in Jill, and the experience had hurt me. I tried to cover up the hurt with cynicism, but underneath, I was scared to be hurt again. That's why I presented you with a business proposition. That way, if the deal didn't work out, I wouldn't be hurt.''

He leaned forward, touched his lips to hers.

Claire's breath caught as his warm breath mingled with hers.

"Claire, I love you. I'm no longer afraid to admit it.'' He drew back, and it was hard to see his eyes in the quickly darkening room. "Do you love me?''

"Yes. But Nick—''

His kiss silenced her. She closed her eyes, slipped her arms around his neck, felt his heart beat against hers. *Nick. I love you. I love you.* The kiss deepened, but before passion could rage out of control, he pulled back.

They were both breathing hard. Boom, boom, boom, went Claire's heart.

"You left me because you couldn't give me a child, didn't you?'' he said softly.

"I—''

"Tell me the truth.''

"Yes.'' Her throat clogged with emotion. She *still* couldn't give him a child. And hadn't he said how much he wanted a family?

"Claire, darling, don't be sad. Whether we have a child of our own is no longer important to me. Nothing is as important to me as you are. Besides, we can adopt. Would you like that? We could adopt one of the children from the home.''

"You told me once you couldn't imagine choosing one child over another.''

"We'll adopt all of them!'' He hugged her close

again, kissing her hair, and Claire closed her eyes, savoring the moment, savoring this intense happiness.

But there were still things she had to know. "Nick, why did you try to prevent me from seeing Brigette?" She had to ask. She was beginning to hope, but she didn't want this between them. They had to clear all the cobwebs away if they had any hope of starting over.

His voice was muffled as he spoke against her hair. "I think in some odd way I felt as if I were reliving my life through Brigette's. I knew about her background. Knew it was very similar to mine. And when you took her for the weekend, it was as if you were toying with her. I thought since you'd abandoned me, you'd abandon her, too. I don't know. It was crazy. All messed up in my mind."

"Oh, Nick." Her arms tightened around him.

"Claire, please say you'll come back. I don't want to live without you."

Claire raised her head. In the twilight, she saw the sheen of his eyes and knew in her heart this was where she belonged. She smiled. "I don't want to live without you either."

And then he kissed her again. This time the kiss wasn't gentle. This time he didn't hold back. Passion flared between them as their mouths and hearts met. And when he took her, only moments later, he took her the same way. Fast and furious. Hot and hungry. Unplanned and urgent. It was the kind of coming together that first-time lovers experience, when they're too greedy and too excited and too impatient to wait. But Claire exalted in its lack of delicacy, its unbridled ferocity, and for the first time, she knew Nick was as vulnerable as she was. He loved her. He needed her. He wanted her.

She reveled in his fierce demand, gave herself up to it, and demanded in return.

She was filled with an indescribable joy, a fierce and consuming love.

When their hearts slowed and they lay in each other's arms, replete, and happy, Nick reached for the music box. He wound it, and the beautiful melody poured over them.

When the song was over, he began to make love to her again—this time more slowly. "Maybe we'll make a baby yet," he whispered huskily.

Claire sighed. "If we were unable to make a baby before, in all those times we made love, the odds aren't good that we will now."

He smiled and kissed the tip of her nose. "You forgot how much I love to gamble!"